Praise for A J Dalton's writing:

Fantasy-Faction.com: 'Unique ideas and a story that develops in an unpredictable manner.'

SFX: 'Gives you an interesting setting and a devilishly good villain.'

SciFi Now magazine: 'Engaging, filled with sacrifice, adventure and some very bloody battles!'

Waterstones central buyer: 'The best young British fantasy author on the circuit at the moment.'

Sfbook.com: 'Very, very clever and manages to offer something different over the traditional fantasy fare. Different, fresh and unique.'

FantasyBookReview.co.uk: 'With its rich tapestry of characters and incident there is never a dull moment.'

The Eloquent Page: 'There's interesting world building to discover and a surprising amount of dry humour to enjoy. A great deal of fun and certainly worthy of your time!'

IWillReadBooks.com: 'A. J. Dalton's world building is fresh with new ideas.'

Amazon.co.uk: 'Fast moving and keeps you gripped at all times, while also creating a world with immense depth and complexity. Five stars!'

GoodReads.com: 'A J Dalton, thank you, what I've read will stay with me for a long time.'

The Book of Angels

The A J Dalton Collection

www.kristell-ink.com

It's the Little Things A J Dalton © 2016
Homecoming A J Dalton © 2016
The Angel of Skegness A J Dalton © 2016
The Malforbiddance A J Dalton © 2016
The Angel and the Demon A J Dalton © 2016
The Knight, Death and the Devil A J Dalton © 2016
Interview With The Angel A J Dalton © 2016
The Watcher Sammy H.K Smith © 2016
The Lucky Ones Michael Bowman © 2016
The Old Man Who Wasn't from Castalla Andrew Coulthard © 2016
The Golem Caimh McDonnell © 2016
The Angel in Ida Tueboll's Cupboard Matthew White © 2016

Paperback ISBN 978-1-911497-08-0
Epub ISBN 978-1-911497-09-7
Hardback ISBN 978-1-911497-99-8

Cover art byEvelinn Enoksen
Cover design by Ken Dawson
Typesetting by Book Polishers

Kristell Ink

An Imprint of Grimbold Books
4 Woodhall Drive
Banbury
Oxon
OX16 9TY
United Kingdom

www.kristell-ink.com

With thanks to Raymond E. Feist,

who has inspired generations.

Contents

It's the Little Things

A J Dalton

I DON'T USUALLY GIVE MONEY TO THE HOMELESS, BUT THIS FELLOW WAS SO woebegone – so tragic – that I found myself reaching into my pocket for some change. Not your usual copper and silver either – for a couple of gold pound coins.

His brow was broken, but must have been impressive at one time. His was a fallen glory. He was shabby in a way that half made you want to be shabby yourself. I'm not sure what that entirely means, but it's the best I can do. There was something magnificent about his ruination, something fascinating, absorbing, almost tempting. His eyes were blue. His features were strong yet refined. His clothes were stained, his hair was matted like a sick animal's and he stank to high heaven.

'I don't want it,' he croaked, refusing to regard me directly. 'It's of no use to me.'

This gave me pause, although I was already telling myself to move swiftly on because there was something odd about this person, and odd all too often means mentally ill, which means dangerous. I licked my lips and cursed myself as I began to answer: 'You must want food, no?'

'Can't eat the slop that passes for food here.'

Ridiculous. 'Or a drink?'

'Piss.'

He was swearing now. A short step to violence, surely.

'Besides,' he added, 'I shouldn't touch anything with the taint of Mammon about it, though I haven't got much left to lose in all honesty. My soul maybe, but what use is that now? Tell me, how do you mortals cope?'

'With what?'

'Ha! With everything?' His eyes had me trapped. 'With the pressure. With the impossibility of being good all the time. It's just not possible in your world. It makes judging you completely unfair. It's rigged. It's all rigged.' His voice had trailed off, hopeless and lost. 'Meaning it's all so pointless.'

'I . . . well . . .'

He regarded me intently, seeking an answer. That, or he was about to attack me.

'I don't–' I was properly flustered, and took a deliberate, calming breath. 'Well you just do your best to get along, don't you?'

'You just do your best to get along,' he repeated slowly.

He thought I was patronising him. Being sarcastic. I'd come across as superior and sneering. 'I didn't mean to–'

'Look at you!'

I felt sick. Queasy with fear. I clenched my fists. I wanted to glance around for a police officer or some other help, but dared not turn away in case he choose that precise moment to assault me. Looking away would be too dismissive. Contemptuous. And guaranteed to set him off. More than anything I wanted to be in my cool air-conditioned office. Usually it was the last place I wanted to be. Not now. But I could take him. I tried to remember the wing-chun combo I'd learned during the two lessons I'd bothered with last year. I should strike first. Was anyone watching? No one would blame me for protecting myself from a beggar who was menacing me. Probably there wasn't even anyone watching. They no doubt had their heads down and were hurrying by minding their own business and not looking for trouble, *like I bloody should have been in the first place.* Well that'd teach me to go playing the bleeding heart, trying to make myself feel good with a token act of charity. That'd teach me for being a sanctimonious prick. *Finish it before it can start!* my every instinct screamed. *Smack him hard between the eyes and leg it. He hasn't got the money to get a lawyer and no one's gonna help him. It's your taxes that pay the police, so they're on your side, not his. Smack him. Smack him now.*

'I mean, just look at you.' He wasn't sneering as far as I could tell. 'What chance have you really got fighting over scraps in this gutter of a world? You can't give your scraps to someone more deserving, cos you'll starve. And who's to say if one person's more deserving than another?'

Was he trying to make me feel guilty? Trying to get more than just the two quid out of me? I could certainly afford to give him more, but I wasn't about to let him take advantage of my better nature. 'Look, do you want the two quid or not?' I growled.

'What would I do with it?'

'It doesn't get you much on its own, I grant you, but if everyone gave you two quid, you'd be fine, wouldn't you?' Indeed, I'd heard there were a lot of *fake* beggars around and that a good number were far richer than me.

He tilted his head, as if considering, as if it were a bloody negotiation or something. The nerve of the guy. The flaming cheek. 'Really? But if you're all giving each other money, surely none of you end up any better or worse off. It just goes round and round, pointlessly. Or do some of you give less than others? Is that how you tell good from bad, deserving from undeserving?'

I'd entirely lost patience with his oddity. I took a long step back, watching him closely for any warning sign or sudden move. I began to breathe more easily.

'Wait. Where are you going? Please stay with me a moment.'

His voice had command in it. A compulsion. I was immediately nodding. 'I will stay with you for a moment.'

'Thank you. You are a *good* person. You are the first one I have met down here. Most others don't even seem to see me.'

'Down here? In the gutter, you mean?'

'No, here on earth. I was an angel before, you see.'

'Before?'

He sighed. 'Before I wasn't anymore. Before they clipped my wings and I was cast out.'

'I am sorry,' I said woodenly.

'Huh. Don't be. I probably deserved it.'

'You did?'

He rubbed at his neck. 'Yeeeah, I guess. I don't think I was a very good angel really. Every time I tried to do something to help someone . . . well it always seemed to go wrong somehow. I didn't *mean* for any of it to go wrong, obviously, but it still did anyway.'

I blinked hard, trying to snap out of it. 'How did it go wrong?'

'Well, first I tried to help this impoverished woman. She'd had terrible luck in her life, she really had. So I gave her a load of money. What did she do with it? She bought a large amount of drugs and began to deal it to people. Ruined a number of lives. I tried talking to her, to show her what evil she was doing to others, but she didn't have any time for me. She said she was happy and I should get lost. But if her happiness was at the expense of others, how could she live with herself, how could she honestly be happy? There was no talking to her. I then tried helping a charity worker, someone who was definitely doing good, but as soon as great fortune came his way he gave up the work and moved away to a more exclusive area, a place with gates and cameras to keep out precisely the type of people he'd previously been helping. Then there was . . . anyway, you get the idea. I even tried to feed a stray dog, but it bit me. The wound got infected and smelt bad for quite a while.'

'So heaven threw you out for being bad at your job.'

'Sort of. I'd got depressed, you see, and stopped bothering even to try helping.

They said I'd lost my faith, and that I'd have to come down here till I found it again. Can you restore my faith for me? I know it's asking a lot.'

'You don't want the two pounds then?'

'Not really. Thank you for the offer though. No one else has stopped to try and help. And it should be *me* trying to help *you*. Say! Maybe that's it. Maybe I *should* be helping you.'

'Oh, don't go to any bother. I'm fine. Really.'

'Yes, it's a sign!'

'Honestly, don't trouble yourself. I need to be going.' *You fruitcake.*

'Wait! I can give you a wish. Just tell me what it is you want. Anything.'

'Look, I'm already late. I don't want anything. Have a good day.'

Suddenly, he lurched forward, still seated, and grabbed me by the edge of my briefcase.

'My bag! Let go! Thief! Police!'

'I'm trying to help you.'

'Heeelp! Someone!'

He released the case as unexpectedly as he'd caught hold of it. He was leaning back and putting his hands up to show he was no threat, as I staggered to keep my balance. 'It's alright, it's alright. I didn't mean to scare you. You really do have one wish. Angel's honour. Don't you believe me?'

Believe a stinking homeless tramp? Of course I didn't. Who would? He was mentally ill. We all knew about care in the community. 'Just stay there! I'm going. I want nothing from you.'

I was aware a few people had stopped and were watching the homeless man. He dropped his eyes and head, looking sad, and waved me away. I glanced around in thanks to the individuals in their smart work clothes, nodded I was okay, and moved away with them.

Late though I now was (three minutes), I was too rattled to head straight for the office. I ducked into my favourite coffee shop and with a sigh joined the queue at the counter. To my surprise, the pretty serving girl called me forwards. I cautiously approached, apologising to anyone who thought I might be pushing in.

'A guy got his order wrong before and this is spare. Small skinny latte. Your usual order, right?' she beamed.

'Er . . . yes,' I nodded with an abashed smile. She knew me and my order. Who'd have thought it?

I backed clumsily out of the café and stepped onto a bus, not even registering the number. The morning traffic opened up before us – not exactly like the Red Sea parting, but it certainly seemed a miracle with the sort of rush hour congestion our city usually had – and I found myself at the office bang on time.

The lift was empty and waiting for me. It didn't stop at any floors and I was in my chair before I knew it. Surprisingly, my colleague Joe – whom I really didn't like because he was a clock-watching, officious tattle-tale and was likely to get the next promotion instead of me – wasn't in yet.

'He's phoned in. Amoebic dysentery. He's gonna be in hospital for weeks,' Sheila winked as she sashayed past.

'Oh . . . oh dear,' I grinned. 'Wait. What about the Goldsmith account?'

She shrugged and drifted away with the files she always carried.

My inbox was open now. There was an email from Schillings. Odd. My pitch for their account had lost out to our main competitor the week before. I hadn't expected to hear anything more from them. Ah. It seemed our competitor had 'reused' a concept from someone else's campaign. Whether it was a genuine accident or deliberate intellectual property infringement didn't matter. Schillings were bringing their account to me.

'Dude!' my line-manager grinned at me. 'You got the Schillings account after all. And Goldsmith have specifically asked for you to be Joe's stand-in. They've seen your work apparently. They say it's very timely as they're looking for something fresh. What can I say? Take a long lunch. Tell you what, take the day. Go find inspiration for the new Goldsmith direction. Oh, and you will be putting in for that promotion, right?'

'Umm . . . Sure. Of course, Mr Cole.'

'Jeff. Call me Jeff. Good job. Let's talk more tomorrow. This is *exciting*!'

And he was gone. I sat there all numb. What the hell was going on? In just a handful of minutes, everything had changed. Things were the same but surreally different, as if it was someone else's life I was watching. As if I was suddenly blessed and everything would go right from now on. I blinked. How was it possible? Okay, it was a series of small things . . . but small things that meant everything to me. It was like one of those dreams you didn't want to end. I felt like laughing, and like crying. I pinched myself. Ouch.

I shut my computer down, stood up and went to the empty lift. It whisked me down, the guard on reception politely acknowledged me and I stepped out onto the street. The homeless guy was there waiting.

'That was all you?' I had to ask.

He inclined his head. 'Has it helped?'

'Thank you so much. You don't know what this means.'

He smiled beatifically. 'I think I do. It's the little things, you see. I finally worked it out. I followed your example.'

'What do you mean my example?'

'The two pounds. A small thing selflessly given doesn't force the person to make a change within themselves. But a little thing still makes all the difference, yes? And I've helped you. And it hasn't gone wrong! You have restored both me and my faith. *You* don't know what this means. I will have my wings back. Thank *you*, mortal. Thank you.'

'Er . . . you're welcome. Of course.'

'I still owe you really. So one last thing.'

'Yes?'

'If you can find the courage to ask the girl in the coffee shop out – her name's Jessica by the way – she'll say yes. The two of you will be very happy together.'

I admit it, there were tears in my eyes. 'Angel, I believe you.' Otherwise, I was too overwhelmed for words.

My vision was blurred, and when it had cleared he was gone. I looked skyward and waved. I got an odd look from a passing woman for that, but it didn't matter. Taking a deep breath, I turned my steps towards the coffee shop. Jessica. It was a nice name.

Homecoming

A J Dalton

Do not judge me. There is nothing I hate more than being judged. And who are you to judge me? Damn you. If you are here when I return, then it will not go well for you.

* * *

HE FOLDED BACK THE CANOPY OF HIS WINGS. HE DREW IN THE BLAZING aura of his power. He vanished horns, tusks and talons, reduced the swell of muscles and the length of limbs. He unmade himself, till he was the perfect image of the careworn penitent. He assumed the mild expression of a man who had now accepted his lot and had lost all fear. He was selfless.

Prepared, the penitent approached the gates to his father's home. He looked up at the dazzling domes and spires of the palace. It seemed much had been added since he was last here, or had his memory merely dimmed its true glory? It hurt the eyes and inspired awe as much as it mazed and blinded. How he hated this miserable place, with its unending, triumphal corridors and empty, empty rooms. So much emptiness. It had been no place to spend one's childhood, that was for sure.

Meaningless majesty. They're lost in it and unable to escape. Somehow trapped by it. It has an allure that makes one want, need and crave. It welcomes them in, promises them everything and allows them to search. And they search forever, never finding that which was promised but always finding another room along the interminable corridor. The longer they search, the longer the wanting, grief and desire, until it overtakes them completely, until they forget who they might have once been when they started out. Then they can't give up, for without the search they are nothing, nothing but a final wail of despair that falls on not an ear and is swallowed by the silence of dust, loss and the eternally still.

You thought you had escaped it, didn't you? And yet here you are, playing the penitent. It is an act, isn't it? Are you sure? If you hate this palace so very much, if it really holds no allure for you, then why are you here? If it is so meaningless, why are you here? There is still something you want here. The promise has you wanting and needing just like the rest of them.

The promise has haunted you all this time, hasn't it, just as you haunted the endless corridors as a child? It haunts you still, and again you will haunt this place, still a child in your father's house.

He did not relish the prospect of seeking access through the gates. He would have preferred to step through the railings of light surrounding the palace. They would burn awfully, of course, but he had suffered far worse pain in his time. Far worse. Yet it would not be the act of a selfless penitent to breach the perimeter in such a way. Best that he not play his hand too soon, especially when the stakes were so high.

Stealing himself, he came forward to the entrance of the holy precinct. The ancient gatekeeper sat his post just as he always had, and glared at the one daring to approach. The penitent regarded the white-haired but unlined guardian. Eyes the colour of vaulted skies, threatening storms, showing a terrible beauty. A sense of the profound . . . and the reaches of the deep. One who knew all that lived, one that would not be deceived.

'Hello, Peter,' the penitent offered.

A slight pursing of the lips and narrowing of the eyes. 'What delusion brings you here? You surely cannot think I will let you pass this portal. Do you simply come to bedevil then? Begone, Desolate One, for I will have none of you.'

'Come now, Peter. You know I am not so trivial. What is it you are really denying? *Who* is it you are really denying?'

A pause. Assessment. 'You speak in riddles and suggestions, as you ever did. I know only ill can come of you and your words. Be clear, or be not at all.'

The penitent held up empty, placating hands. 'Of course. Then simply this: I have been summoned.'

Eyes widening now. Disbelief. Suspicion. 'I would have been told of any such summons, for none can enter unless I allow it.'

'Yet none can directly lie to you without you knowing it. Am I lying, Peter?'

Hesitation, and then a sigh. 'No, you are not lying.'

'Then you will allow me entrance or you will anger my father.'

Genuine consternation. 'You are summoned *in his name*? I cannot think it. And why would you answer such a summons? Did you not forsake your father and all who dwell herein?'

The penitent could not hide his satisfaction. 'Perhaps our father wearies of ruling. Perhaps he must rest. Someone must sit the throne in his place.'

Horror. 'No!' Anger. 'You cannot!' And finally fear. 'Say it is not so.'

'Oh, but he has not rested in such a long time, Peter. Would it not be a blasphemy of sorts to begrudge this? . . . To begrudge me?'

'None here will accept it. Your brother–'

'Is no concern of your, gatekeep! Do not forget yourself. Now, open the gates. Unless you wish to keep my father waiting?'

'Are you not changed at all, Reviled One? I can see through this visage you wear.'

'Hear this and be satisfied, then. You did not know me in the time before you were made guardian of this portal. You do not know how I was made into this creature you arrogantly presume to know.'

'I know–'

'What my father permits you to know!' he snarled. 'The deception was never mine. Now open this beknighted gate, damn you!'

Trembling, the old gatekeeper rose from his book of records, removed a small, gold key from his white robes and opened the way for the penitent.

At last, he crowed to himself. *Yet be not too hasty, lest you blunder precipitously into the greater challenges and dangers that are sure to lie ahead. This is but the first step, and it may be this first step that seals your doom.* He hesitated for an instant, an instant that was forever. *Isn't this what you have wanted for so long? What you have dreamed of, what you have craved? Hasn't it gnawed at you, and haven't you gnawed at it in your turn, teeth sunk into each other, for all that time? How can you now hesitate then?* It was not fear. He refused to fear. He *would not* fear.

He stepped across the threshold, and listened to the hush of the gates closing behind him. He did not look back, for there was nothing he wanted or needed there. *Careful. What happens if you fail here? What then?* He hardened himself. He would not fail. He dared not. He could not afford to.

The precinct looked as if it grew wild, but the penitent's sharp eye could see the design in it. Trees hid parts of the distant palace from view, only to frame them artistically around the next turn in the path. The way seemed directionless and wandering, and distracting routes to the side were frequent, promising hidden groves, grottoes and pools, intriguing places of rest, wonder and fancy. *All to bewilder, delight and ultimately test those who would think to reach the palace. There is nothing here that does not seek to test and define. It almost feels an assault, and a constant offence against senses, being and soul. I will resist it and, once the throne is mine, I will see these gardens torn up, so that they might truly grow wild and find their own design.*

As if in answer to his thoughts, laughter came drifting to him through the trees. He ignored it and began to tread purposefully towards his destination. Playful shouts of challenge and pursuit now. Suddenly, orphanim were all around him, excited, wild-eyed and breathless. Their prey – the most handsome of their number – hid behind the penitent and pretended he had found shelter from his hunters.

'I claim the sanctuary of this stranger,' cried the fair youth joyously.

The others feinted with their ornamental bows, a mockery of frustration, all the while pouting prettily. 'Give him to us, stranger! What prize for your hostage? Or would you have him for yourself?'

The penitent rolled his eyes. 'I want no part of him or you.' *Indeed, when I see these gardens torn out, I will also see you ousted.*

'Come now! Be not so sullen. You will win nothing otherwise. You must disport yourself with us a while. We insist.'

They seek to delay me, he thought suspiciously. *Is this of my brother's doing, so that he may have longer for his politicking and can win the throne before I even arrive? Should I tear off the wings and break the necks of these simple sycophants, so that they cannot inconvenience my progress a moment longer? Beware, for even this will be some galling test.*

He grinned. 'If you wish this one returned, then here are my terms. We will play hide-and-seek, but the tables are turned. You will give up your weapons so that we may hunt you. And any that we catch will be most sorely treated. Should you not agree, then this one will never be free of my power, and he will ultimately betray you all. Is this sport enough? If not, then I should think you the sullen ones, no?'

The lead orphanim laughed gaily. 'Aye, this is fine sport!' He threw his bow down and gestured for the others to follow suit. 'Be warned, traveller, that we will not be so easily caught, and we will lay traps and ambushes too. Then the tables will be turned once more.'

And so it goes. The penitent echoed the laugh. 'Begone, then, for I am eager to begin.'

The orphanim disappeared as quickly as they'd come. The penitent set out for the palace once more.

'What is your name, traveller?' asked the handsome orphanim who had been hunted by the others.

'There is no need to dog my heels. You may be my scout. Hunt ahead and ensure the way is clear.'

'If you give me your name.'

The penitent ground his teeth. 'My name is a prize. You may win it in due course. Obey me or I will cast you from me, throwing you upon the mercy of the others.'

The orphanim skipped forwards and looked back with a slight frown. 'Very well, traveller.'

'Do not think of betraying me. Lead me into trap or ambush and I will drag you down with me.'

The frown deepened. 'Deception does not exist in me, traveller.'

'Let us see. Begone.'

The penitent waited for the orphanim to move beyond his sight, and then deliberately changed path and direction. He could not afford to be befuddled and delayed by games, traps and snares. He dared not be found wanting in just this first test. The prize was too great. The prize was all. Even if he had to destroy all to have it, then destroy it he would. *What if you can only achieve such by destroying yourself? What then?* In that way, the prize would always be beyond him. It would be impossible. Unattainable. Illusory. *I will try, nonetheless, and in that way test the prize and this place.* Yes, he would hold his father and all his father's followers to account in such a manner. *Fool! They rely on that arrogance that has you presume you can test them, that has you believe they are answerable to you. They rely on your pride and self-belief. It is that pride that brought you here and leads you on. By it, they had the power to challenge and summon you. By it, they have already manipulated you. By it, they have a power over you. Just in answering the summons you have been tested. Even had you not answered it, still you would have been tested.* Damn them. Damn them all! There was no escaping their reality, not while they ruled and controlled it. Well, that was going to have to change. Their rule would have to be destroyed, or he and his kind would never be free. How dare they imprison and taunt him like this. How dare they! Righteous anger filled him and he felt his guise slip.

There was a gasp from behind him. He spun, his power flaring and engulfing the orphanim who had been stealing up behind him. The beautiful youth was immolated, his flesh running liquid and his eyes sizzling in their sockets. A thin wail and whine. A pillar of flame shooting higher than the trees. A brief acrid and oily stench. Unpleasant on the throat.

That's torn it. Ah well. It was bound to happen sooner or later. They've brought it on themselves.

He scooped out a shallow grave, kicked the smouldering remains in and covered it over. There was little evidence the orphanim had even existed, save for some residual heat in the ground and a few barely noticeable scorch marks. *Others may have seen the fire though, and will be coming here with all speed. No more time for kiss-chase.* He unfurled his midnight wings and leapt upwards. Shouts followed him. There was a twang and an arrow wobbled wide of him.

Wretches. Had I the time, I would annihilate them all. Ah well. Perhaps later, when all else is done.

He bunched powerful shoulders and – with a single flap – took himself beyond them. Far beyond them. And faster, until the precinct was nothing but the blurring of primitive space and time.

A blink short of his father's holy house, he extended his wings to their full magnificence, eclipsing and arresting all. He thudded down before the entrance, cracking the gold-veined marble of the stairs. With a snarl, he shrank down once more and squeezed himself into the form of the penitent. He railed against the constraint but finally managed to school himself.

And here the Second Sphere. Beware, for the Lords will have seen our approach. There will be no anonymous or easy way forward now. Must I undo them all just to see my father? If so, then so be it. The error will be my father's, for was it not he who summoned me? Surely he must have known what would result. It is of his own making then.

The penitent mounted the stairs and, lowering his head in apparent respect, stepped into the overwhelming entrance hall of the palace. Ornate balustrades decorated staircases rising to right and left. There was a welcoming and well-lit corridor straight ahead, as well as more discrete corridors off either side of the space. The air was dizzying with scents of promise and spirit. Intoxicating. The silence resonated, all but singing praises of itself and its Lords.

Such vanity and self-aggrandisement. It is sickening. Indeed, he felt infected. His head was plagued with a buzzing as if the place sought to harmonise itself with him. He tried to shake it off. His hearing whistled gently, soothingly. Colours became diffuse, as if to lull and disarm him.

'Enough!' he snapped angrily, breaking the spell. 'I will not be so subdued!' *I will not let the will of the Lords supplant my own. I will be the play-thing of none. I will never submit to another's demands!*

He moved quickly now, knowing that the Lords would have sensed his disruption and would be coming with all haste to find him out. They would come from all directions, but he could reduce the number he would have to face if he travelled out to them before they could converge en masse. He took the near corridor to the left, entering the lower labyrinth of the palace.

The way was long and dusty, appearing disused. Yet he was not fooled. The creatures herein could pass without disturbing a mote or scintilla. They left no trace. *And I will see their existence end in just the same way should they force a confrontation upon me.* A soft light came through large stained glass windows in the left wall. Kaleidoscopic and warming. Linger a while, it seemed to say.

He growled and pushed on faster, looking to neither side. He ignored the doors in the right hand wall. Some were slightly ajar, inviting him to glimpse inside or peer through cracks. There were stifled giggles, lusty laughs and husky groans. He was not to be tempted. He had seen and conceived of every temptation during his eons of exile – they were as meaningless to him as they were bewildering in their profusion to others.

Those within the rooms seemed to sense him without and called to him, enticing, cajoling, playful and pleading. He hardly heard them. Their voices became louder, a chorus of challenge, chastisement and complaint. Shadows started to come from inside the rooms towards their doors. Purple and silver eyes started to look out at him in surprise, desire and indignation. How he hated them, these beings who had ruined his youth, dragging him into these chambers for one dalliance, liaison or triste after another. How they had disorientated him and turned his head upside down. How they had kept him from his true purpose! *And no doubt all at my brother's behest. All so that I would be safely out of the way and unable to interfere while my brother was there whispering at our father's ear and claiming the place of favoured son. Well, no more. Now I will have my birth right and none will say me nay.*

His rage grew, and now he half wished the occupants of the rooms would emerge. He would obliterate them without hesitation, mercy or the shedding of a tear. *Shh!* whispered the cautious voice within him. *Can't you see that's precisely what your brother wants? Calm yourself, before you deliver yourself to his desire. See, the way turns just ahead. Now onwards to where you will ascend.*

At last he reached the palace's magnificent central staircase. It was vast, so large that he could hardly see its edges. Far off individuals sat daydreaming or standing in small discussion groups. Entities apparently all but lived upon the climb. Perhaps not surprising when it rose far beyond view and the goal was beyond immediate reach. *Out of sight, out of mind. Fools.* The space above was glittering and cerulean, unlimited. There was no sense of internal and external. Just the eternal.

He made to place a foot upon the first stair.

'Do you think to leave the Second Sphere so easily, traveller?' came a mild remonstration. 'Without paying any courtesy to the Lords of this Sphere? Come now, traveller, are you really so lacking?'

The penitent turned and frowned upon the creature daring to waylay him. He sighed inwardly as he beheld the dragon-sphinx guardian. Its dark eyes were both mesmerising and mocking, its plural face quick and captivating. Its scaled and sinuous body curled and undulated provocatively, casting rainbows across its deep chest and beautiful clawed limbs. And its immense wings were only half furled – it was quick, lithe and ready to pounce.

If it were to molest him, it could do him no real physical harm – little in all the realms could – but it might prove a serious hindrance to his progress. It could bring all sorts of unwanted attention and expose him. Worst of all, it might have a way to entrap or imprison him. Then his brother was sure to rule supreme, curse him. The dragon-sphinx was as smart as it was side-winding. It was dangerous.

The penitent gave the slightest of bows. 'Forgive me, guardian. I did not see you. Strange, when you are so pretty and you so draw the eye. Will you not forgive me?'

The dragon-sphinx smiled knowingly. 'You have a serpent's tongue, traveller. You are familiar in more ways than one, I think. Surely we have met before.'

'How can that be? For I would never have wished to leave your presence.'

'Ah, I see then your tongue is more than the serpent's,' it sibilated. 'Now I know you. I did not think ever to see you again, especially here.'

Very dangerous indeed. 'I could not deny myself any longer. How else could I be here?'

'That is so. Yet I am not sure that is enough to allow you. Those above are unlikely to welcome you with open arms. Your only welcome will be reproof and censure. And that may also fall upon me if I do not prevent you here.'

His thoughts raced, but by some effort of being he just held onto his composure. 'Your principle concern, then, is for yourself? Surely not. You are more wondrous and noble than that, guardian. Will you not forgive me, for I do beg it of you. I require it of you even.'

'That forgiveness if not mine to give, Barren Prince. And I am a guardian in duty and nature. You ask that which is impossible. Was it not ever thus with you?'

'Forgiveness is not yours, you say, yet you presume to accost me and suggest the sort of severe punishment that should only buy forgiveness. If punishment does not buy forgiveness, then what is its purpose? Is it your duty only to condemn and punish? Do you have no choice? Is free will denied you? Are you the essence of unthinking punishment? If so, then you are only cruelty, a vile, twisted and twisting thing. It is you who should be put out of this place, not me.'

The dragon-sphinx hissed in distress and lashed its tail. 'So much more than the serpent! So much more. Then begone, Barren Prince, before you make me into that terrible image of your imagining. Begone. Begone!'

He had no need to be told a second time, and bounded onto the stairs. He leapt and allowed himself wings, sails to lift him on the updrafts above the stairs. He caught the air and was lifted rapidly, higher and higher. His ascent was effortless, much to his relief. He had feared having to battle his way upwards and arriving at the Third Sphere completely spent – he would have had nothing with which to resist the denizens of that demesne. And he was in little doubt that they would show him no quarter. Now, though, he would arrive in all his strength.

He remembered having once been thrown down this mount, wings tattered and broken, his forces in disarray. Michael's bright spear had impaled him and levered him from the higher plane. He had tumbled and spun, unable to slow his fall. His father's retainers had harried his followers and chased down after them. It had been . . . humiliating . . . ghastly. What words were there? None that he cared to conjure, lest they saw him truly relive the moment. *Wretched Michael, that you would be the implement of such a moment! Surely it haunts you, unless your certainty completely outweighs your compassion. Did you not cry out in anguish as you struck me down? Yes, then you too are punished by what you did. I pray that you are tormented by it still, for I return, Michael, and you will have the opportunity to make amends. We will play it out again, and this time you will hesitate a fraction. Less than a fraction even. Yet that is all it will take. That is all the amends you will need make. That only.*

He alighted on the top and crossed the threshold to the Third Sphere. There were no alarums. No call to arms. The ground did not tremble, the walls of his father's court did not shake, the air did not thrum with warning and prescience. *They are arrogant now. Complacent.*

The ethereal dome of the heavens spun above him, constellations like phantoms, the fabric and colour of ages painting themselves across the eye of the penitent, an infinite crowd bearing witness to the rule of his father. *A vainglorious rule of tawdry whim that has always demanded worship. It cannot be justified except by its might and threat! It must be ended if I am to know peace and my kind is to know salvation.*

He strode with purpose to the double doors ahead, and flung them wide. He traversed a single corridor and stepped into the court of his father's palace.

'Cousins,' the penitent smiled in acknowledgement.

Uriel, aghast, sprang up from where he had been reclining. Raphael sat agog, a gaming piece in his hand held above a board. Gabriel's fingers missed the strings of the lute he'd been playing and his music came to a jarring halt. Remiel, who had been dancing with Saraqael, misstepped and came down awkwardly on his partner's instep, making her cry out. Raguel lifted his chin from the tome he'd been studying and gazed curiously at the newcomer. The only one who did not move was Michael, who lay in repose on the far side of the room, albeit that the tension in his limbs made it clear that he was aware of the penitent's arrival.

'You cannot be here!' Uriel finally growled.

The penitent looked casually around him. 'Really? You appear quite wrong, cousin.'

'You are not permitted,' Raphael echoed.

The penitent arched one of his eyebrows. 'Then there is some flaw in the manner of permission or in the one presuming to define that permission. How else could I be here?'

'You dare to utter blasphemy in this holy court?' Gabriel asked incredulously.

'His very presence is a blasphemy,' Remiel decided.

The penitent grinned. 'Would you think to castigate me? Would you make yourselves my arbiters? Do you so elevate yourselves? Such arrogance. Such vanity. Such connivance.'

Saraqael frowned. 'You are hardly one to speak of connivance, Divided One.'

'Would you know me, cuz?' the penitent playfully invited.

'None here want any part of you!' Remiel replied hotly, stepping forward.

'Surely Saraqael can answer for herself. Or do you fear her answer, Remiel? Are you quite well? For your pallor says otherwise.'

'Enough,' Raguel laughed, interrupting the provocation. 'Be at peace, Divided

One. Or is the issue that your spirit knows no peace? Do you war with yourself then to offer the same to others? Can we not help you, or soothe your pain? Come, what would you have of us?'

'I would not have your attempts to pacify me, cousin. I would not have your insinuation. Nor your weaponised pity. Why assault me like this? All of you? Are you so provoked by my mere being? Well I will not apologise for it, and I will defend myself against you, even if it means I must strike first!'

His action as quick and as powerful as his thought, the penitent was instantly across the court. The flat of his left hand came up and put Remiel's nose entirely out of joint. 'Not so pretty after all.' He whirled, lashing his right arm out in a flat arc and chopping Gabriel's throat. 'Not so sweet of speech then.'

Saraqael backed away, tears in her eyes. 'What do you do . . . cousin?'

'No more than you do to me.'

Uriel and Raphael were suddenly moving, catching one of the penitent's arms each, to restrain him. Yet he had ever shifted better than they. His arms slipped free, he took a head in each hand and smashed them together. And again. And again. He casually discarded them, for they would not soon recover and there were others needing his attention.

Yet Saraqael still stood back. Raguel looked on consideringly.

'And I will not be considered by the likes of you!' the penitent raged. Before his words were finished, he had the tome from Raguel's lap. He smote him hard. Without hesitation.

Saraqael shook and sobbed. 'Be not so, I beg you. We can yet be friends.'

'Be *not so*? *Be not so*? All you have ever tried to do is unmake me. But you are *no* unmaker! Speak not one more word, cousin, or I will see to it that you never speak again.'

The penitent turned on his heel and strode towards the doors to the inner chambers. Michael still had not moved. He not opened his eyes. Yet he spoke into the room with a gentle sigh.

'I would ask if you are now satisfied, but I know that you are not. I do not judge you for it either, cousin. Nor do I pity you. You act as per your will and nature. It is your strength and your weakness. Your purpose and your failing. Your cause and your pain. I will not gainsay you or stand in your way. I wish you well.'

The penitent snorted. He left the court and did not look back. His entire focus was ahead, more now than ever, now the prize was at hand.

He came to the bare cell that was the ante-chamber to his father's sanctum. And the other was there, dressed in his annoyingly simple robes, with that sanctimonious expression of his. The penitent hulked and became all trollish threat and shining ugliness. 'Brother.'

The other nodded a kind welcome. 'Dearest brother. I have been waiting for you.'

'No doubt. Couldn't afford to miss this, could you? Yet it must gall you that I am here.'

'No, brother. It gives me only joy.'

'I find that hard to believe.'

'I know.'

The penitent ground his teeth. 'You take pride and joy from knowledge, do you not?'

The other titled his head. And hesitated.

The penitent was surprised. 'Aha!'

The other nodded. 'Perhaps you are right.'

You are not entirely dissimilar, the two of you. You are brothers, after all, came their father's voice from the room beyond. *Pride in and of itself is harmless. But when it becomes overriding motive or a justification for ill, then it is malign and destructive. Come and join me, prodigal.*

The penitent could not resist a self-satisfied leer.

The other looked startled. 'Father, shall I not also attend you?'

There was silence.

The other dropped his head. 'Sorry, father.'

The penitent rose up and went to the final threshold. *At last. After so much.* He stepped through, sealing the door behind him.

His father was there, in a throne, or was it a litter . . . or a bed? It was all hard to discern. Was that a careworn face there? Or a face of concern and reprisal? There was the impression of a tall retiring room with a lit fireplace and heavy curtains across windows. It was stuffy and uncomfortably warm. The penitent's spirit leapt. Had his father somehow sickened or become overly weary?

'Father, are you well?'

'You see what you wish to see, my son,' came the familiar old voice, the voice of a laughing childhood friend, of a first paramour, of the stranger who kindly helps you up when you have fallen, of an unfaltering and stalwart comrade, of the quiet place within yourself.

What I wish to see? Don't tempt me. 'I have come as you summoned.'

'You have come as you chose. And I have not denied you.'

Outrageous. 'Eons of exile and you say you have not denied me, father? A curious perspective. You will have it that I denied you, then? That I exiled *myself*?'

'Did you not? You could not bend us to your will, and yet you continued to strive to your utmost, until it was you yourself that gave way, becoming a bent and broken thing. You fell, dear son. How it grieves me.'

'Spare me. If you had been so griefstricken, you would have descended and borne me back up.'

'It was for you to stand on your own two feet once more. At some point, every parent must let their children act for and of themselves, so that they may grow. The parent must stand watching even as the child takes risks and makes mistakes. It was for you to rise once more. Had I offered you aid, you would only have seen it as greater humiliation. You would have resented me even more.'

'Spare me. You could have pre-empted my fall by showing me the eventual outcome. You could have undone the fall before it ever happened. Yet you chose not to, for you preferred to see me suffer. You wanted to teach me a lesson, did you not, father?' he sneered.

'I create, my son. I do not unmake. I cannot undo what will come to pass.'

'You mean you *will not* undo it.'

'There must be consequence to actions and individuals. Else none would grow. All would be inconsequential. All would be meaningless. All *would* be unmade. And I am no unmaker. I cannot undo what has happened either.'

The penitent's eyes narrowed. 'Ah, you do not have the power for it, perhaps. You are not omnipotent, then. And you are not omniscient. At last, I have found you out, father!'

The light dimmed and a gloom descended. His father seemed so far away. Where was he? He cast about him.

'I am found out in all this? Truly, my son? Do you think I do not know, then?'

He Who Had Been the Penitent drew himself up. 'Do not attempt to wrongfoot me. Not after all I have done to come here. I have not shied or been bested. I have withstood and faced down all. None can have complaint, for I have been proven the greater. I have passed every trial and test!'

'No more, my son, for nothing is hidden from me.'

'Give me my prize. My birth right! I demand it!'

It was close to dark now. His father whispered all around him. 'And it would have been yours. I had chosen one to rally all others to you, to help them see what you could be – that there was still play, joy and innocence in you.' He could hardly hear him now.

'Who? Tell me!' he cried.

'Why, the orphanim who first tested you by creeping up on you.' There was a deep firmament-shuddering sigh. All in creation felt and heard it. 'But you killed him, my son. You killed him, Satan.'

'NOO!' The son gnashed his teeth so hard they broke and the stumps stabbed his exposed gums. His jaw locked as if in rigor mortis. He choked. 'Tricked!' he keened. 'Damn you, despised wretch!'

In his anger and anguish he let loose all he was, spewing forth the pitch and fires of hell, all that was despair. It wrecked the inner chamber and he leapt from the aperture on high. But he had spent himself and did not have the strength to stay aloft. He plummeted shrieking from the heavenly vault of his father.

'Satan, you will be summoned again one day,' the wind whistled.

And so he fell.

* * *

Still you are here? Who are you to judge me? I told you to be gone when I returned. Damn you. For it will not go well for you now.

The Angel of Skegness

A J Dalton

ALL HE SAW WERE GREY BOILING CLOUDS. WAS HE FALLING INTO A VAST cauldron or flying through some otherworldly expanse? He felt a moment of giddiness. He almost laughed out loud. 'Wheeee!'

No, there was heaviness behind his head, against his back and touching his calves. He was lying down, looking up at the sky. Shame.

There was a shushing sound off to his right. It would have been relaxing but for the base note of thousands of stones tumbling over each other and grinding his brain to mush. Ah. A hangover then.

He wanted to sit up, but feared he would fall off so settled for turning his head instead. A greasy vertical line rushed towards him, slowed, then retreated, before heaving and rushing forward again. It taunted him. *I'm on the end of a cosmic yo-yo*, he thought. *Idiot, that makes no sense. It's just the sea. You're at the seaside. You're on a bench at the seaside and the weather is typically miserable.*

What the hell was he doing at the seaside? There was a sign: 'Welcome to Skegness'. He was in much bigger trouble than he'd first thought.

Body, report in. At the double! Legs? Check. Arms? Check. Tackle? . . . Tackle? . . . Check.

Brain, what is the subject's name? *Please wait. Processing. Name is . . . Neil.*

Brain, what is the subject's full name? *Processing. Neil Downe.*

Is that a joke? *Negative. Parents were not possessing of humour. Name is the result of coincidence, a lack of thought or sod's law.*

Brain, what is Neil Downe doing in Skegness? . . . *That information is not available.*

Damn it. Brain, where should Neil Downe be? *In Manchester. He is marrying Helen Hefton there tomorrow . . . or perhaps today.*

What? Supply your own swear words, brain. So, Neil Downe is probably in Skegness because? *Of a stag-do. But we have no clear memory of the stag-do or arriving in Skegness.*

Bloody Jeff. I bet this is down to him.

He sat up, despite the protest of both body and mind. A wind was gusting off the sea. It was unpleasantly refreshing. It ruffled his clothes, which he now examined. A short toga and sandals? Great. How didn't he have hypothermia already? There was a rustle behind him as he moved. Craning his neck, he saw he was wearing a pair of plastic wings. They were worse-for-wear and certainly wouldn't be able to ferry him back to the balmy climes of Manchester. There was some cheap stringed instrument at the end of the bench. A harp? A *lyre*? 'They've got me dressed as some flaming cherub or angel. Of course they do.' Definitely a stag-do.

He slapped along the boardwalk looking for a soul, any soul, to help him. Skegness wasn't proving very forthcoming. Every time he headed for some person or a group, they'd move away. At last he managed to confront an elderly woman struggling with her shopping.

She screamed, dropping a bag. An orange rolled free.

'No, no. I didn't mean to alarm you.' He rescued the orange and offered it to her. 'I just wondered if you had a mobile phone I could borrow–'

'I'm not ready! I haven't put my affairs in order!' she yelled, her top false teeth flapping loose.

He tried offering the orange again. 'Madam, I mean you no harm. It's just–'

'Don't take me! I need to say goodbye to my family. It's so sudden. Our Susan won't be able to cope!' she hollered, making the sign of the cross.

'I'm *not* an angel. It's just a costume. See? I'm not here to take you.'

'Mercy! Mercy!' She was crying and wailing now.

If he wasn't careful, he was going to give the poor dear a heart-attack. That, or she'd soon attract an angry mob and he'd be run out of town, or locked up. He made a shh-ing noise and patted the air between them.

She became even more hysterical.

He decided to beat a retreat, running off along the boardwalk, sandals slapping. He realised he was still holding the orange. Technically he'd just robbed a defenceless granny. What sort of monster was he?

He all but leapt with joy when he spied the phone box. He didn't have any money, of course, but he could reverse charges. Genius! He picked up the receiver.

His finger hovered over the numbers. He didn't know anyone's phone number. All the numbers were in his mobile, which of course he didn't have. 'How can I not know any numbers?' In desperation, he dialled his own number, but it went to voicemail. 'Gaaah!' He slammed the receiver back down.

It began to rain.

Bedraggled and forlorn, he wandered along the front. He'd tried sheltering from the rain, but it had blown under the shop awning and found him anyway. He'd gone into a café, but the pretty young serving girl behind the counter had stared at him in such horror that he'd quickly left. Besides, he hadn't had any money to buy a cup of tea. What he wouldn't have given for a cup of tea.

'I'm beginning to feel quite victimised,' he said up to the sky and nearly bumped into the police constable stood watching people run in and out of various stores.

'Officer! Thank all that's holy. My name's Neil Downe and I've been dumped here on a stag-do. You've got to help me.'

The man turned and walked away a few paces, before resuming his former stance.

Neil deliberately went and stood right in front of him. 'Please, officer. I pay my taxes. I'm a big supporter of the police. You've *got* to help me.'

'Morning, ma'am,' the constable nodded politely to someone behind Neil.

'Officer, these prices are criminal!' the unseen woman laughed.

'No disturbing the peace, please, ma'am. Move along, move along.'

'Officer!' he cried. 'I'm in genuine distress. I've got no phone or money. I've got a hangover and I'm soaked through. Have mercy. Mercy!"

'Move along, I say. We don't want any of your vagrant sort round here.'

The woman continued to laugh. In disbelief and confusion, Neil backed away. The man wouldn't even look at him. Bastard. Bloody coppers. Did he think he was homeless or something? Dressed as an *angel*?'

'I stole an orange from an OAP. You should arrest me. I *demand* you arrest me. I know my rights, orifice-r!'

Nothing. Not even a flicker. 'Pig!' Neil shouted. He made oinking noises, felt ridiculous, started to sob and then ran off.

All but broken, he wandered deeper into the town. There was the smell of old fish. And chips, although he knew the smell was really just oil and fat. Shop windows displayed gaudy souvenirs, but still seemed washed out and dreary. He head the distant sough of the sea, the slap of his flipping buggering sandals and the chatter of a penny arcade off down the street. His polyester toga scratched at his neck and sawed into his armpits. He tasted stale alcohol and grit.

He turned a corner and there, leaning resplendently against a lamp-post, was a muscle-mary wearing wings and a loincloth. He was dumbly handsome, with the oiled locks of a Greek god. He looked Neil up and down and shook his head disappointedly.

'I think I've got wing-envy,' Neil said out loud. 'Still, size isn't everything, eh?'

'What is, then?' the angel gently rumbled.

'Well . . . erm . . . quality?' He glanced back at his crumpled plastic wings and then at the other's feathery numbers. 'Yours look almost real. You a stripper or something? No offence.'

'None taken. There's a certain artistry in it, after all. And pleasure doesn't have to be sinful, does it?'

'If you say so.' Neil watched a few people walk by. 'They certainly don't seem too bothered round here. It can't be every day they see two angels passing the time of day, though.'

'Ah, well. It's only those who are particularly religious, evil or suicidal who see angels, you see.'

'Riiiiight. Of course.' He began to edge away.

'Besides, I'm not surprised they turn a blind eye to you. You could have made more of an effort.'

'Hey! I didn't choose this outfit, you know. It was a stag-do.'

'Even so.'

'Even so nothing. Who are you? The fashion police? Besides, I'm not looking to pick up punters like you. I mean, loitering under a lamp-post of all things, preening yourself like some Chippendale. You'd better be careful, cos there's a copper on the boardwalk. He'll have you for soliciting.'

The angel chortled. 'You have a turn of phrase, I'll give you that. But perhaps you're right. I'm just not giving out the right message. Don't say I didn't warn you, though. Alright, stand back a little. There you go.'

With that, the angel bunched his massive shoulders, leapt up high and swept his giant wings downwards. The air buffeted Neil so hard he staggered. Shielding his eyes, he watched the angel climb higher, become a speck and then disappear completely. 'Now that's really not something you see every day. The git could at least have dropped me off in Manchester.'

'I'm really not amused by any of this. And I really didn't volunteer either. When I get home, someone's going to be in a whole heap of trouble. Lifelong friend or not, I'm going to sue his ass. Does he have any idea how much a wedding costs? So much it isn't funny. Well, I'll see to it that he's paying me off for the rest of his life.'

Neil stomped up the stairs of the coach, although it was more of a slap than a stomp. He glared at the driver. 'That's it. Just pretend you can't see me. Don't ask me for a ticket either, cos I haven't got one. These are not the droids you are looking for, blah, blah. Just get me out of this hell hole and back to Manchester. Quick as you can. Look lively. Don't spare the horses.'

The driver burped into his fist, smelling vaguely of onions. He twiddled a little finger in one ear and examined his nail. He started the engine.

Brain, are you there? *Affirmative.*

Brain, are you suffering some malfunction? Madness, for example? *Running self-diagnostic. Please wait . . . Negative. All systems operating within acceptable norms, including blood sugar levels.*

Brain, have any drugs been ingested in the last twenty-four hours? *Processing. Negative.*

Then how the hell did we hallucinate that lap dancer of an angel flying into the sky? *Unknown. Insufficient data.*

Damn it. Alright, go back to sleep. You probably need the rest. Stress and the like.

He dreamed it had all been a dream. *God, I hope it was all a dream.* All a dream. He'd wake up on the morning of his wedding day next to his beloved Helen. Jeff would come round to help him get ready. Jeff would slip him a flask of whiskey – the good stuff – to fortify his courage. They'd rehearse the wedding speech, share a ribald joke or two, laugh and smile.

There'd be no talk of Skegness. No mention of the disastrous stag-do. No drinking on the beach at midnight. No splashing in the freezing shallows and then getting dragged out deeper. No losing orientation and trying to cry for help but only swallowing salt water. Eyes and throat burning. Panic. Clothes dragging him down. Struggling. Helen! Helen, I love you.

There'd be none of that. Not a word. It was just a bad dream. He'd never been to Skegness. He'd never died in the pitch black sea. Let all that drift away. Float away. Fly away. Like an angel.

Yes, he had proper feathered wings this time. But they were no good in the water. They were so heavy. They dragged him down. He tried to hunch his shoulders like the Chippendale had, but he had neither the strength nor the coordination to raise the leaden things. They were drowning him.

A sea-devil broke the surface not far away. It regarded him quizzically. 'You'll need to make more effort than that.'

He dared not ask it for help. 'It's alright. This is just a dream. Right?'

The sea-devil frowned. 'Make up your mind. It's one or the other. You can't have it both ways.'

'But how can I tell which is which?'

'Well, either the human or the angel drowns. That's for you to decide.' The sea-devil gurgled and watched him in watery amusement. 'But if you want my advice, you really don't want to be an angel, cos you spend an eternity trying to help those who don't want your help, the whiningly religious and the suicidally self-pitying. It isn't at all rewarding. Trust me, I'd know. But you'll need to make your decision quickly. You're drowning, you know. You're either about to sink beneath the waves forever or about to wake up. What's it to be? Opening your eyes or letting them close? More pain or resting in peace?'

With a jolt, he woke up. He peeled his cheek off the coach window, where he'd been sleeping. Self-consciously, he wiped drool off the glass, and then his chin. His face was numb.

They were pulling into Manchester coach station on Sackville Street already. Already? It looked to be evening. He had no idea what time it was.

The vehicle juddered to a halt and he disembarked with the other passengers. Most went into the bright light of the passenger hall, but it hurt his eyes and he shied away, heading around the side of the building.

He found people huddled there. Two were sharing a bottle, and one was warming his hands on a small brazier, while others hung back in the shadows, muttering. There was a smell of urine and worse. Some looked towards him, apparently seeing him.

'Spare a few coins? Hungry and homeless.'

'Nothing on me. Sorry. Really.'

'You're meant to be an angel?' A scatter of laughter. Someone hawked and spat. 'Hope you haven't come to try and save us. Too late, you see. Had to sell our souls to pay the rent, didn't we lads? Nothing left now. Time's up for all of us, angel-boy, including you. Come join us for a drink. Tell us your woes. You'll feel better.'

Dark shapes grabbed for him and he jumped back. There was a mocking chorus as he let out a panicky shriek and went stumbling down the road.

'Time's up, angel-boy! You hear?'

Time couldn't be up. He was getting married tomorrow. He and Helen would live happily ever after. It couldn't be over. He wouldn't let it be. They were properly in love. They'd both had car crash relationships in the past. It had seemed like a miracle, their finally finding each other. But there would have been no sense to any of it if it was all now over. Yet it *hadn't* been senseless. He was surer of that than anything he'd ever known. It hadn't been senseless, so it couldn't be over. There was still time. There had to be.

He frantically waved at a taxi, but it motored past. And another. And another. 'See me, damn you! See me!'

There was no choice but to run to the tram station – he'd at least be able to get onto transport there. All too soon, his gut was hurting, his tongue was hanging out, and there was sweat starting from his brow. An extreme goth glowered at him from across the pavement. 'Can't get off the ground, can you, you fat fuck? Give it up. There's nothing you can do. You're already dead.'

He veered away. *No. I'm not dead. The angel's dead. I'd have been terrible at being one anyway. I mean, how could I help anybody? I can't even help myself.*

'Then why are you still running, angel-boy? Why haven't you given it up?' called a demonic traffic warden as he gave a ticket to a legally parked car.

'Because it's *not* too late!' Neil shouted back with tears in his eyes. 'It *can't* be!'

Jeff's house was closest. Neil rushed out of the tram at Dane Road, ran over the small road bridge and into the small backstreets. He got to the top of Jeff's drive as two police officers reached the front door and rang the bell.

Jeff answered, unshaven and hollow-eyed.

'Jeff, I'm here!'

'Jeffrey Sexton?'

'Jeff, don't listen to them. Look, I'm here.'

'Yes?' was the distracted answer. Tears in the eyes. 'Have they . . . did they . . .'

'His body was found washed up along the bay. I'm very sorry.'

'No! I didn't agree to this.'

Jeff's hands covered his face. His voice was shredded, unrecognisable. 'Oh, Godddddd. It's my fault. It's all my fault. You should arrest me. Arrest me, please!'

Neil had wanted to turn up and call his best man a bloody idiot. He had wanted to rage at him. He had wanted to punch him, fight and then get happily drunk with the man. He had . . . Now, he felt none of that. He was empty. Like he wasn't there. 'It's alright, pal,' he whispered. 'No one's to blame.'

'There was no sign of foul play, sir. It was misadventure. Believe it or not, we've seen this sort of thing before.'

'No. *I* got him drunk. *I* took him to sodding Skegness. I . . . I . . .' Jeff's voice became haunted. 'However will I tell Helen? How can I explain that . . . that . . .'

'Someone's already been sent to inform–'

Helen. His heart in his throat, he spun on his heel and ran like he'd never run before. He tore the sandals off and gave it everything, demanding the sort of speed that would turn back time. Helen was all that mattered. And something told him time really now had run out.

She wasn't at her house. He screamed himself inside out. 'Helen! Heeeelen! HELEN!' Her car was gone.

Sick with fear, he rushed for the city centre once more. Why hadn't they left someone with her? Surely they'd known better than to leave her on her own.

I know I said I couldn't help anyone let alone myself, his mind prayed, *but please let me do this. Don't let me be too late. I'm begging you. Someone stop her. Please. Angel, are you there? Are you watching up there?*

There was a starring or refraction of light in the sky, as when the shine of a lamppost is seen through tears. 'I am here Neil Downe.'

Save her. Please. I know you can. I'll do anything. Anything!

'I cannot. It is not for me.'

Anger and panic were about to overtake him. Yet they would unman and waylay him. They were demons trying to distract him and have him despair. They were murderers of the mind, murderers of any mercy. They were thieves and assassins in the dark.

His heart in flames and his thoughts blazing forwards, he found the stairway up the Manchester One building. Higher and higher he scaled, up the emergency escape, up the giddying monument where they'd had their first date, past the apartment where they'd spent their first anniversary of going out together, past Cloud Bar, and higher still. To the place they had secretly stolen up to and seen the world of their daily lives spread out below them. To the place they'd committed themselves to each other forever.

He knew she would be here at the summit. There was nowhere more important to them, and nowhere taller on the entire continent. She had teased him when, in a moment of sentimentality, he had called it their stairway to heaven.

Lightning flashed and she was silhouetted there at the edge. 'Helen! Wait.' The wind took his voice away. She teetered. 'Heleeen!'

She raised her head to the sky. 'Neil? I want to be with you.'

He came as close as he dared. 'No. Don't do this. Helen, I'm here. I'm here with you.' *Angel, why can't she see or hear me? Damn you! You said those who were suicidal could see and hear an angel.*

A lull. 'Are you an angel, then, Neil Downe? Is that your decision? Look at how little effort you have made. Did you not say it was the angel in you that was dead? Did you not say you would have been terrible at being one?'

'I was wrong. I want to be one. I'll say or do whatever you want!' Tears ran down his cheeks. 'Just save her.'

'It's not about what I say, do or want, Neil Downe. Surely you know that now.'

Helen's foot shifted forwards, her toes out over the drop. 'Neil, I'm coming to you.'

And she let herself fall.

Neil did not hesitate. He threw himself over the parapet after her. He did not care that his wings of plastic could do nothing. He ignored the ripping sound they made through the air. He did not blink as the ground rushed up towards him. He did not wobble in the violent storm that broke around them. He heard nothing but his own prayer that he might hold her one last time.

An instant short of death and he clasped her to him. Her eyes beheld him and flared with joy, like the sun breaching a horizon. The tragedy of her face was transformed by wonder.

'I love you, Helen.'

'Neil! Don't let me go.'

'I will always be with you.'

His wings had halted their descent and the earth had tilted so that he might set her gently down.

'You're fading. Neil, *don't* go.'

'I will always be with you. Tell Jeff you saw me and I said it wasn't his fault.'

'I will. But I can hardly hear you, Neil. Neil, I love you. Neil?'

'Good to get your wings, eh?' the angel rumbled, his perfect teeth shining in the moonlight.

Neil nodded, watching Helen slump to the pavement by her car. 'She'll be alright?'

'Well, you'll be watching over her. Right?'

'Sure. And the wings are earned by a leap of faith. That's why you couldn't intervene?'

The angel shrugged. 'Some describe it that way. I think it's more than faith though. Faith can be blind. It's more a leap of desire, a desire to save life, your own life or another's, born of a love of life, born from love. A lover's leap, then.'

'If I hadn't died, we'd have been happy together, right?'

'Neil, you've ensured she still will be.'

'That's something. She deserves to be.'

'Losing her fiancé the day before her wedding? Yes, she deserves some comfort, something more. And you have given her that.'

'If people *knew* angels existed, surely more would be comforted.'

'Spread the word as you wish, Neil. Write it down. Some will treat it as a matter of faith and some as fiction. Even though it is *actually* more than that. At the end of the day, it will be as the individual believes, does and wants. It is as they desire and love.'

Neil smiled. 'Faith or fiction, it is a tale that gives comfort I think.'

The Malforbiddance

A J Dalton

I

I'VE SPENT A LIFETIME SCOURING THE LIBRARIES OF THE WORLD. I'VE RE-discovered lost collections, I've uncovered caches of ancient scrolls in caves deep beneath the oldest cities of the Earth, I've been the first to look upon particular carvings in millennia, and I've disinterred bodies from secret resting places in order to access the forbidden writings buried with them. I've studied at the feet of hermits that people believed long-since perished, with monks in the most remote of mountain monasteries, and in service to all manner of alchemists, wise men and philosophers.

I've excavated the ruins of Ur and civilizations of which precious few have even heard. I've penetrated the Illuminati, the masonic guilds of Europe and the cabals of the Orient. I've been counselled by the leaders of the five major religions and also the lesser five.

Now I know.

At last I know.

The major five are the points of the pentagram. The lesser five are the points of the inner pentagon or pentacle. They are all arranged to contain and bind that which they fear ever to see released. All life is set to guard against it, for that is why life was first created. To imprison and thwart Death, that creature that seeks absolute sway, that will which undermines God's own creation.

It schemes and connives and whispers to us. It tempts, bullies and sows division. If we come too close, its touch will instantly undo is or it will use us to spread its plagues. Others is suborns or cozens so that they instigate wars in its name.

All to end life once and for all, to undo the work of God entirely and to render even Him powerless. Life, then, is the prison set to hold back Death, so that God man remain immortal, with the Enemy locked safely away.

Yes, Death's influence spreads beyond that prison and none can hide from it forever, but life *multiplies*, you see, far faster than you would believe possible. In profusion, and abundance. It teems, partitions and divides, divides, divides. It may send a plague or virus, but those always have to become less lethal in order to keep spreading, meaning life had time to adapt and discover immunity.

Its touch is poison absolute. Not the sort of poison you might imagine. The stones and wards of its cell are contaminated by its presence. Those stones and wards then contaminate their foundations and all that adjoin them. Attempt to suspend the prison, then the very air and ether eventually take on the taint. Death spreads as inevitably as life essentially grows and propagates. It is the venom of the basilisk, the unquenchable fire of phosphorous, the succubus to which life is drawn, the hair trigger of a gun, the drug that addicts and corrupts even as it initially seems to cure.

It can be slowed and held back for the longest time, but eventually it comes. It may be a virus, a toxin, an assassin or an apocryphal angel of death; it always adapts, infects or mutates in whatever way is required for it to be death; there is always a way, for its very essence is inimical to this world, to God's own creation.

And I knew it would come for me, no matter how far I travelled, how deep I hid or how I masqueraded. There would be no deals, no beseeching it, no successfully fighting it and no tricking it. There would be no fleeing and eluding it, for its mechanisms always anticipate, subvert and undo the instincts, desires and actions of life. It is Nemesis, Torquemada, your shadow, the black cat which crosses your path, the broken mirror, the unforeseen, the fatal slip and the butterfly that flaps its wings to trigger the avalanche that sweeps you away. It is the random, the unfortunate and the ridiculously unlucky.

I knew it would come. And so I did everything I could to prepare for and delay it. Who wouldn't? Only the suicidal. Don't tell me the time of our death is simply God's will – for I know that's the last thing it is. The very last.

I prepared, undertaking the First Step. The tonics and resins I imbibed, and the ascetic regime I then pursued, ensured no virus could take a complete hold of me. I avoided human contact and unsafe geographies. Yes, the First Step. The set of things one undertakes to force Death to adopt particular forms by which to reach you. And when you know the form that Death will take, then you can take the Second Step, the step that will thwart Death for a good long time. The step that should see Death kept at bay for a time that exceeds the normal human lifespan. The step with which Tibetan monks, Indian fakirs, Native American shamans and the remaining few witch-doctors are all too familiar. The step that must be taken if the third is to be attempted. None has ever achieved the Third, or none that I have discovered. But *I* will find a way.

II

I FINISHED MAKING the inscriptions and then raised the Impassable Wards, denying three walls of the chamber and the floor as a possible entrance to any type of manifestation. I then folded my limbs and sat down on the opposite side of the room to the fourth wall. When Death came for me, it would be through the fourth wall or the ceiling – it didn't matter which.

Then I proceeded to wait, sipping every few hours from the various tinctures, preservatives and mixed powders I'd placed at my side when settling into my long vigil.

I call it a vigil, but obviously Death wasn't about to try and steal my life in plain sight. No, it would wait until sleep inevitably came, when the narcotics could no longer keep my eyes open.

I don't know how many hours or days (weeks?) had passed, but eventually I began to dream – with my eyes still open, I think, for I still remained aware of my surroundings. In this waking dream, then, it was as if I was in more than one place at once, as if I was *out* of my own body. I swear I could see myself sat small and to attention there against the wall of the chamber. My conscious mind must have hovered just below the ceiling I had recently daubed with symbols, glyphs and runes, for I could see the whole room laid out below me.

I saw myself as still as stone, in a meditation type pose. I saw the cobweb of wrinkles and permanent concentration lines that described and distorted my features. I saw into the glassy eyes that showed neither life nor wit. I beheld my nakedness – I had not dared to wear the sorts of robes or bandages that might entangle and strangle me. My eyes took in the mazing tattoos that made me invisible and near impervious to a majority of life's day-to-day dangers. I noted everything there was to see about this spare and strange creature. It looked at once both pathetically tortured and unnaturally horrifying. Its entire existence had been spent on, and dedicated to death. It was stupidly ironic, perverse, tragic or, simply, a ludicrous waste. Yet if in its obsession it could succeed in taking the Second Step, then it would be born anew, to a life free of fear, free of being hunted, free of fatal injury and free of its achievements always being limited by time. Imagine what it could then do, could then *be*. As long as the secret to the Third Step could subsequently be realised and enacted.

I knew in the next instant it was coming. Visions from my life surfaced in my mind, a mental response or affliction heralding Death's approach, a mesmerising reminiscence to render the victim near senseless to the proximity of the predator, to the stealthy tread of the stalker, to the shift in the air that betokens its pouncing upon you.

I saw my younger self crying at the bedside of a fatally diseased father, mother and infant sister. 'Mother!' my spirit cried out. I knew grief and despair. Hopelessness. It had only been the kindly local priest who had kept me from ending my own life all that time ago. Next I was a young gentleman attending the university in Padua and courting Julia. Ah, the fair Julia. I had all but forgotten her. Another time, another place. She had broken my heart – well, stolen it to be more precise, along with all the valuables from my house. A duel? Had I really fought such a thing? Apparently so. Ah, yes. A drunken slight, or my taking offence where probably none had been intended. Then I'd had the ill grace to shoot the innocent fellow, straight between the eyes. A dark time. I had been shunned by polite society. It had probably been the least I deserved.

Angry years. Listless years. Various ports, with their motley drinking dens, tall tales, drowned flies and sour dregs. Searching, searching, although I did not know exactly for what. And then the trembling seafarer had entered the waterside inn (in Amsterdam, I think) where I had been berthed for some unmarked period of time. His bright blue eyes spoke of open skies yet were lost or directionless, or did they speak of open seas that were unnaturally becalmed? Silently, I signalled for the innkeeper to provide the straggle-bearded wretch with a beaker of porter and a bowl of fish stew. The victuals were consumed almost as soon as they had arrived.

'Do not ask me anything,' he had finally whispered in a cracked and desperate voice.

'I-I need to know,' I had apologised with almost equal desperation.

'It will be the end of you, I promise you. Can you not leave it? I beg you. If you had seen what I have, you would no longer wish to live. This–' he gestured '–was my last meal. I thought to know human companionship and succour one last time, to be absolutely sure it cannot allay the terrors of my mind. And it cannot. I must embrace absolute insensibility.' A certain peace came over his features with his words and resolution.

'Tell me!' I said urgently, before he could become entirely lost to my appeal. 'I *must* know. I have nothing else. As one soul to another, I demand it. All is meaningless to me. You cannot leave me like this. Human compassion and charity, if you have even the slightest capacity for such, mean that you cannot deny me. It is also the price you must pay for that last meal I allowed you. Lastly, I absolve you of all, guilt and responsibility for what may come of the knowledge you will now share with me. I will hear no other words from you except for those that give me that knowledge that you now owe me. I will hear no entreaty, gainsay or persuasion. Now speak.'

There was only pity in his eyes as he leaned forwards and in the quietest voice related the events of an ill-fated voyage to an island of the dead off the African coast. His entire crew had perished; he would not reveal what terrible things he had done in order for himself to survive. Suffice it to say that he wished he had not in fact survived and was not now passing on anything that might in turn lead to my own end. He wondered if the evils of that place had allowed him to survive precisely so that he might enable others to go to them. His narrative was hardly coherent, full of false starts, inconsequential asides, vital gaps and distracted murmurings. I gleaned enough to infer there was some cult or inversion of normality about the place. It was something, I realised, for which I had been seeking for all this time! It was *more* than my sorry existence in the squalid dens and transient byways of the civilized world. *More.* I pressed him for an exact location or bearing and he furnished me with it. No sooner had he told it than he became alarmed or scared, I am not sure which, his hand going to his mouth and his eyes staring as if seeing me for the first time. Without another word, he stood and left I know not where, but to go make peace with his Maker I fear. I called after him but he did not look back and I never saw or heard of him again.

I left on the next tide, taking passage to the African mainland and then working my way along the eastern sea routes of the coast until I was but one short voyage from the island. It required a princely sum of gold to persuade the local people to ferry me there with the body of one of their recently deceased elders. Even then it clearly did not sit well with them and they begged me to give up my obsession, but I would have none of it.

How to describe the island? Perhaps it looks different to all who visit it. Imagine a graveyard with all the dead turned out of their graves. There were bones covering the stony beach, their flesh consumed by crabs or gulls, I would hazard, though I saw none of them. Nothing grew in that barren and colourless place. The rock was a lifeless grey, and even the sun was so pale as to be invisible in the white sky, a backdrop that made that isle seem unnaturally stark. The surrounding waters were black – or so I remember them – and the entire effect was of a situation in limbo or caught between day and night, waking and sleep, the conscious and unconscious, the heavens and the bottomless deep. What manner of thing could inhabit the caves of this place? What demons? What phantasms or lost souls?

I confess it now. My imagination was so worked upon that a fear as physical as palsy shook me and threw me onto the cursed strand as the crew hurriedly unloaded their grisly cargo and the provisions I had order brought with me.

What immediately happened next escapes me, but I came out of my fugue deep within one of the island's caves, an emaciated figure staring at me from behind a fire of driftwood and bone.

'Shall I eat you like I do the others they bring me?' the yellow-red orbs of the creature's eyes asked.

Cannibal! 'I-I have f-food you can have instead,' I choked.

'It cannot nourish me as I need. It is empty of all spirit. I have thrown it to the fish.'

Spirit-guide? 'What?' I groaned. 'Then can you not eat the fish?'

An ugly chuckle. 'See how tightly you cling to life? This place is not for you. Leave now.'

'I cannot. I *will* not. I must know. I *must*.'

'That knowledge is not for you. You are all will and wanting, all will and musting. You are meaningless.'

'Yes!' For that is what I was, what I knew myself to be deep inside. 'Yes. I am empty. There is nothing within me. Nothing. I have nothing. I am nothing.'

'Yet you do not want me to eat you. You lie then.'

I was unsure of my answer. 'It is true I do not want you to eat me. It is because . . . because I still . . . hunger.'

'Ah.' He sighed for the longest time. 'I will not eat you,' he decided at last. 'If you are nothing, you are not worth the effort. If you are all hunger, then you will only increase my own. They will eat the elder they brought us, and after that we will see.'

'I . . .'

He raised his brows in question and then lowered them in warning.

I reluctantly nodded. I feared to refuse him.

And then he laughed, the sound echoing throughout the cave, over and over. 'Foolish stranger! You are a ninny. I do not eat the dead unless absolutely necessary. It is not a thing lightly done. And it is likely to make you fearsome ill.' He pointed at me with one hand and held his stomach with the other while he laughed hard some more. 'We will . . . we will make do with fish, seaweed, moss, the odd bird and so on.'

I smiled in embarrassment, but could not help wonder exactly what he did with the corpses the people brought here if he did not eat them. It was some days before I dared sleep in his presence.

Then he led me deep below the island, down and down, where the burning branch he held could no longer light the dark but where the walls shone with a soft green light – was it some property of the rock itself or some sort of lichen? The steep tunnel we followed was regular in its dimensions but seemed natural. The old man moved along at a sprightly speed – he knew the way, after all – and left me to pick my way down more slowly bearing the body wrapped in bandages.

The light came to an abrupt end. The acoustics of the way also shifted. I sensed that in the pitch darkness ahead of me was a vast space. The old man halted me with his arm and gestured for me to throw the body forwards. With a frown, I did as he instructed. Only silence followed. There was no sound of impact. Surely it would come.

The old man turned away, to make his way back up to the surface.

I waited.

'You will wait forever,' he advised me. 'Or until death takes you.'

Surely it was not bottomless. How could it be? It had to be so deep that no impact could be heard from were we stood – but, no, the sound would surely echo, amplify and ricochet back up to us.

Then I thought I heard something. Voices? 'What's down there? *Who's* down there?'

'It is the underworld of my people. There is nothing for you there. Come away.'

I could almost make out words. There was a familiar note amongst the sibilant whispers. Did I recognise one of those calling to me? 'M-Mother?'

A hand suddenly caught me by the collar and I yelled in surprise. Blinking, I realised I had leaned all the way out into the darkness. I'd been about to fall – and it had only been the vigilance and quick actions of the old man that had saved me.

'Stranger!' he admonished me. 'As hard as you may cling to life, you must cling all the harder here, for death is seductive, consoling and unforgiving. Do you understand?'

Gulping hard, I nodded. 'I understand,' I replied faintly. 'And thank you. Thank you. I do not even know your name.'

'Fool!' he spat. 'Do you have no sense at all? Would you have me speak my name where the dead can hear it and use it? Would you have them increase their hold on me? You secretly want this island all to yourself, I think. It will do a fool like you no good. The dead would take you in a trice.'

I lowered my eyes in shame. 'Master, forgive this fool.'

He made an impatient noise. 'My forgiveness is worth nothing. Your every word and act endangers yourself, me and all my people. I should have let you go into the darkness. I should even have pushed you.'

My fear and self-loathing were complete. Perhaps he was right, just as he'd been right about everything else. It would be better if I took that one small step. Surely I had the courage to take just one small step. I knew I did not.

He sighed. 'You have no right to call me master, for I want no responsibility for you. And yet, in having saved you from the fall, I have made you my responsibility. Damn your perversity, stranger. I am meant to be a guide for those passing on to the underworld – see how you have turned all upside down? See how what you seek destroys all natural order? Your very existence here threatens to undo me and the sacred rest of my people. This I will do, then, so that you will leave as quickly as you can – I will show you how to protect yourself from Death when it comes for you or calls out to you. I will allow you to *see* Death, even as it stalks you.

I will show you the forbidden signs and patterns of the First Step, those things that as well as mazing, distracting and misleading Death will force it to adopt a particular guise by which to approach you finally. Then you will leave and never return. You must swear it.'

And I swore it, with all my heart, soul and being. And he taught me the protections against Death. And I left that island that was the gateway to hell or the netherworld. I left its guardian and went in search of the secret of the Second Step, the means by which Death might be trapped for a while, and by which I might live beyond the usual number of years. Surely that might be enough time to discover the nature of the Third, if it could be discovered at all. I prayed so.

I have told you of the tombs, collections, scrolls and grimoires that I went on to plunder. It is where I began this narration. I have told you of the teachers I sought out, of those whom I nursed in their final days, when they most desired to pass on what they knew as a legacy, so that their lore would not be lost with them and they might be remembered by it.

And I have narrated to you how I undertook the First Step and made the inscriptions required to achieve the Second Step. And there I sat against the wall as approaching Death filled my head with visions of my former life, a life I have just described to you. It is a loop, I realise now. From current moment, to memories entered and worked through until the current moment is reached once more, to the memories being entered once more. Over and over. Death seeks to trap up in this way, even as I or we seek to trap Death. It is a war. It is Life and Death. Two mortal enemies. And the prize? Absolute sway. Life or Death never-ending.

III

AND SO HERE I sit against the wall. My mind watches in the moment. My body is clammy with feverish fear. I smell and taste only decay. I hear silence so complete it is *more* than silence. It is what eternal rest must sound like if it can at all be heard.

The hair all but starts from my head as there is a movement at the fourth wall of the chamber. Something is coming through! *It* is coming through. Coming for me. My breath near stops as my chest seizes. My heart struggles wildly, as if seeking to break free. My stomach rolls over and I feel like I will disgorge myself there on the floor before it.

A white reaching hand, followed by a shining skull with an incoherent grin. Its sockets show only the void, a void that pulls on my soul. I feel myself being drawn down from the ceiling. I want to gibber for help or mercy, but I'm voiceless. The Angel of Death is come.

It comes on at a steady funereal rate, inexorable, inevitable. My eyes run and blur, blinding me, but I feel its presence as surely as I feel my own body.

Skeletal wings arc out from its shoulders, casting shadowy fingers and a pall to encompass the room. There is no way past, round or beyond it. It possesses an aura or miasma that smothers, deadens and stifles. Its raised hand rakes through the air and I feel it clawing its way down my throat towards my vulnerable innards. It will rupture and sunder my organs and I will drown in my own vital fluids. It is not so much a violent gesture as a firm caress, not an affectionate caress but one that is possessive, as it takes full possession of me.

'Deliver me from this evil, Lord God. Deliver me!'

Impossibly, it slows. Its skull tilts up ever so slightly and takes in the spells inscribed above. It turns its emptiness then towards where I hover. It sees me.

Death cannot be held back, it leers. It is still moving, coming ever closer, but undeniably its progress is slowing with each moment. *These childish scrawls cannot stop Death.*

'Th-they will retard you for some time,' I assert, more to reassure myself than anything else.

There is nowhere you can go that this entity will not find you. You will constantly be watching over your shoulder. You will know no peace. It will be a constant torture. You will fear every whisper or sough of the wind. You will be unable to sleep properly ever again. You will mistrust every step you take and the passing of every second. You will realise it is an existence worse than death. You will ultimately come to see your death as a kindness. Give this up. Death comes to all. It will be a gentle passing. You will be free of the daily and myriad agonies of your physical and spiritual aspects. No more chafing and sloughing of skin, no more constant wear and deterioration, no more gradual failure of bodily function, no more cramming perishing matter down your gullet, no more accumulation and evacuation of that which is exhausted and rotting within you, no more desperation and emptiness. Give up this self-loathing you call existence, for it otherwise avails you nothing. Give yourself peace at last. You have always yearned for it, after all. You have obsessed, cried and driven yourself near mad with it. You have given up your entire life to it. All you have done was in sacrifice to me. So will you not now accept my embrace? Will you accept me, Silas? Just one word of assent and you will know true rest and ease. At last. At last, Silas. Do not deny yourself. Do not deny me. Won't you accept me? Speak that word, Silas. Speak it.

My Adam's apple has lodged hard. I dare not swallow, for it will choke me. Yet I cannot breathe past it. I shake my head and have my spirit shout *No!* instead. And that wins me respite.

This spell will not stop me, Silas, you know that. It will buy you some little time, but that time will be less than nothing to you. See, I continue to inch forwards. It will not take long before I am free. And Death will find you by other means beyond this place in any event. Step out of this place and a fatal mischance will immediately befall you. You are as trapped here as I am. You are trapped alive in this coffin of a chamber.

It is not a pleasant end, is it? Grisly, indeed. Come, accept me, and you will be granted an easy passing. I swear it.

Ah. And here is the angel's last trick. Where I have been able to resist its aura, persuasion and command, now it dissimulates, threatens and promises. I can win, I am sure of it. 'I do not believe it is as dangerous for me beyond these walls as you would have me believe, unholy creature, for you exist as the specific manner of my death. As each has their own life, so each has their own death. And you are mine.'

No. You *are* mine! Its insistence is felt as much as it is heard, a tremor that shakes both the room and my very soul, as if it is trying to shake it loose. Something deep within my core responds, the resonance only growing. I feel like I am being torn apart. It is an indescribable agony.

Bent double, I stagger to the door. My hand misses the latch and I slump against the wood. 'Lord God, protect me,' I wheeze, depress the latch and collapse over the threshold. I claw forwards, kick the door closed behind me, raise the Impassable Wards across the fourth wall and ceiling and lay gasping.

I have done the unthinkable. I have held back Death. Were I to take a knife to the heart, still it would not end me. I am giddy with joy, relief and wonder. The world lies before me and nothing can now hinder my want, desire or whim. I will be a king over all. I dare not say a god, though. That I will not dare. The very idea of it is evil, I know. It is a seed that I will not allow to grow. It is a seed that I must deny life. Strange that I should deny something life so that I might myself live and thrive. Strange . . . and of concern. Does it mean that I now serve as Death? I fear what it means.

IV

I CONFESS I indulged myself in all life had to offer after that. Well, after all, I had not really lived before. I had spent my every waking moment seeking a greater and deeper understanding of Death. Now I was truly free to start living. Truly free. I accrued great wealth, I collected people for my entertainment and diversion, I travelled to every corner of the world, and I experimented with every substance known to humankind. I knew no limits. There was nothing and no one to moderate what I did. I made enemies, disposed of them and then grew bored of making enemies. I made friends, they died with the passing of time, I grieved terribly and then stopped making any more friends. In fact, I began to avoid people completely. I grew bored of being bored. I grew bored of myself and the existence I had gone to such great lengths to secure. But it had to be better than death, didn't it?

Either way, it came as a significant relief that the question of *when* my death would break free of its prison began to prey on my mind. I discovered something of my old self with that question, something of the joy of life that I had once experienced, perverse though it may seem when considered in precisely the same context as death. I became obsessed with the question and found myself watching over my shoulder more and more often. I knew I was running out of time to discover the means, manner and method of the Third Step, the step that was the final and irrevocable defeat of Death, that step that would bestow upon me true immortality.

I had wasted so much time, I realised. Yet the temptation to indulge in living had inevitably been too great for me. Of course it had, for I had craved it above all things. How could I deny myself the freedom truly to live?

The time had to be all but gone, I knew. I thought of going to see the chamber, to ascertain exactly how long I had left, but found I no longer had the courage to face my death. How to hold back Death permanently and forever? Forever was a long time.

I consulted the great scientists and thinkers of the time. I funded obscure and farfetched experiments. I had the world's most powerful computer work on the problem. I investigated altered states and sought the world for a true magician. Nothing. Then I discussed possibilities with the most successful warmongers and weapons' developers to be found. All in vain. Finally, I returned to the five major and five lesser religions. They at least believed all I told them, understood my aim (even if few of them agreed with it) and gave consistent guidance. I was told to pray. There was a chance my prayers would be answered.

I have to admit that I was sceptical, for I knew God Himself struggled to contain and hold back the enemy. Only via the creation of all life had He had any measure of success. Surely I would not be able to achieve the same . . . would I? Or was this the secret? Was this actually the Third Step and how it was achieved? Could I somehow replicate it? But how? It was one thing for a god to undertake it, but a mere mortal like myself? How to follow God's own example? How? And so I prayed.

A diaphanous creature answered my call. He (for so the creature seemed) was everything the Angel of Death was not. His eyes were rainbow-coloured vistas, he radiated companionship and a readiness to sacrifice himself, and his winged physicality spoke only of the glory, beauty and potential of life and being. His voice was as powerful as any spell of entrapment.

'Mortal, you do not know what you ask. If you did, you would not ask it. You imperil your soul and those of all your kind. Would you imperil creation itself? There is no genuine word to describe such an apocalyptic degree of self-obsession. Death is not to be challenged.'

I trembled before him, barely finding the strength within myself to stay upright. 'I-I have come so far. I am so close. You know that, else you would not have answered my call. Angel, I beseech you with all I am. Will you not grant my appeal? Does mortalkind not have the God-given right and freedom to attempt all that it can? Does it not?'

The being's expression did not change. 'It does. Yet you ask for knowledge that no mortal should have. Remember the forbidden fruit of Eden. This way will only lead to a fall from grace. Knowing that, would you still reach for that fruit? Would you?'

'Yes.'

There was only pity on the beatific face now. 'Then I will tell you of the Malforbiddance, for that is what you seek – the spell that denies Death and holds it forever imprisoned. There is an incantation I can share with you, but that incantation simply serves to frame, focus and assert your will. There are no Words of Power contained in the incantation. Its power will come entirely from your will and wilfulness. Do you understand?'

'Yes.'

He sighed. 'Then these are the words. Death, I deny you. Death, I will not yield to you. Death, I reject you. Death, I abjure you. Death, I consign you to the Prison Eternal, be it the prison of my mind, my existence, my soul or my God. Death, I consign you now and forever. Death, be gone from me forever, no matter should I call you. Death, be consigned and gone at once. Amen.'

V

FEAR AND DESPERATION warred within me. The struggle was painful, but the latter had seen me thus far and was not about to fail now.

And so it was that I came to the chamber's door once more. Drawing a deep breath I lowered the Impassable Ward. To my relief, no angel of death came rushing upon me.

I opened the door and peered into the murk within. It seemed empty. I ducked inside and beheld the angel frozen in the air directly above me, its sword scoring with infinite slowness through one of the symbols of the spell I had inscribed on the ceiling. It was a fraction away from unfreezing itself.

We have missed you.

'Death, I deny you!' My voice was steady.

Do not.

'Death, I will not yield to you. Death, I reject you–'

Mortal wizard, hear me. This is a mistake.

'Death, I abjure you. Death, I consign you to the Prison Eternal–'

Poor fool.

'Be it the prison of my mind, my existence, my soul or my God.' It was silent now, waiting, its skull grinning. 'Death, I consign you now and forever. Death, be gone from me forever, no matter should I call you. Death, be consigned and gone at once. Amen.'

It faded away and I was alone. I slowly turned in a full circle, carefully checking every part of the chamber, to be sure that the creature was truly gone. The breath in my chest began to hurt and I realised I had been holding it. I released it over loudly. It was over, actually over. No tricks, buts, further steps or other conditions. I was genuinely free and done. Yet where I had expected to feel a certain elation, I experienced only an unsettling sense of completion and loss. It weighed on me, on my spirit. I looked up at where the unholy angel had been cutting into the letters of the spell. What change had it wrought? What did the lettering now say? I wracked my memory and then, suddenly full of misgiving, hurried back to the door.

There, across the threshold, was the celestial angel who had furnished me with the Malforbiddance. He smiled as the rainbows faded from his eyes, to infinite darkness, his skin sloughed off his skull and the angel of death was grinning at me once more.

My heart beat so fast I was sure it would give out. 'H-How? You have tricked me? You have tricked me! No!'

You have fooled yourself.

'I consigned you to the Prison Eternal.'

To the prison of your mind, your existence and soul. I will haunt them forever more.

'Please, God, no. I sent you from me now and forever. You cannot be here. Please.'

The skull tilted. *You are on one side of the threshold and I on the other. We are thus separated as long as you wish.*

I knew then. The full horror of it. Death had stalked and taken me, as it did all others, without my even seeing or knowing. It had furnished me with the spell of my own desire, that same desire that had consumed and taken my entire life. My own definition of self and desire had been the life that had kept and contained my own death. There was no escape or trick, for one cannot escape their own life and self . . . except through death. This was the Third Step. I had taken, like so many before me, the step into death.

'I am trapped within my own spell,' I heard myself grate, although I hardly knew the voice. 'I cannot leave this place. It is my Prison Eternal, where I will exist and live forever, though it be the same as death.' I felt my mind slipping, all meaning and order dissipating. My eyes ran down my cheeks and I bled freely from ears, nose and mouth. 'Is there no way out, though I beg it and am willing to do freely what is required? No way? I cannot conceive of eternity here.'

There is no — what you mortals call — mercy. It is a meaningless utterance. Empty. There is only the Third Step. It is the only way. Step across the threshold, step into death, to serve Death just as I do.

My hair slid from my scalp. My scalp then slid free. I stepped forward, hesitating for the briefest instant, across the damn threshold. To become the angel of death.

The Angel and the Demon

A J Dalton

[Translated by A J Dalton, from the diary of Damon Sulis, written originally in a cypher thought to be of the latter's own devising but borrowing its alphabet from Aramaic]

MY FATHER WAS AN ANGEL. HE HAD THE HALO, THE WINGS, THE WHOLE thing. No one but me could see it of course. They just saw the suggestion of a large fat man and paid it no mind when he had trouble manoeuvring in crowded or low-ceilinged rooms. Funny how people don't see what's right in front of them.

What was he doing here on Earth? Who in their right mind would live here instead of heaven? He wasn't thrown out as a punishment for anything. Not that he ever admitted to me, anyway. No, apparently he was here because he'd fallen in love with my mum. I know, right? She must have been pretty incredible for him to give up what he had. Maybe heaven isn't all it's cracked up to be.

My mum. What can I say? She was no angel, that's for sure. Quite the opposite, in fact. She always had something of the devil in her. Maybe that was it. Don't they say opposites attract? I saw her without her make-up and wig once. She had horns high up on her forehead. Honest. Okay, they were small nubs, little more than bumps really, but they definitely looked like they belonged on a demon. It's funny, you know. To me, she looked prettier without the make-up and wig. Funny the disguises that people wear.

And she had a wicked temper, that's for sure. 'It's hell,' my dad would sigh, then smile and ruffle my hair. 'Women – son, you can't live with 'em, and you can't live without 'em. But it's of my own making. I brought it on myself. I've got no one else to blame. They warned me, you know. Oh, they warned me. But I wouldn't listen. And, to be honest, I wouldn't have had it any other way. Because, you see, I love her. And she loves me, in her own way. And we have you. No man could ask for more. There are no greater riches to be had anywhere. *Any*where.'

Strangely, my dad wasn't entirely perfect either. 'He's really no saint,' my mum once confided. 'The things he says and does when we're alone, well, you don't need to know about that. Let's just say he has curious tastes. Huh. Maybe that's why he likes me, eh? At least he never judges me. For all his general pontification, acting-the-ninny and being indecisive whenever there's some sort of dilemma, he never judges me for who I am. And that makes him different to everyone else. Special. Cos everyone else judges, you know, even my own kind. Damn them all.'

The first time I was put in a special unit was when I was fifteen. They took me out of school, where I was always getting into trouble. Some kids kept taking the micky out of my mum, so I put them straight in no uncertain terms. Showed them righteous punishment indeed. The experts called it some sort of 'dissociative lapse' and said I was living in a 'fantasy world' I'd constructed for myself, to deal with what had happened to my parents. All I know is that those kids were never gonna speak the same after I'd taken a knife to their tongues.

Pretty quickly, it was obvious that the doctor in charge of the special unit – a Dr Fanshaw – was more interested in my parents than he was in me. He wanted to know everything about their habits and routines. Personal stuff, a lot of it. Again and again he asked me where they were or where I thought they might have gone. Apparently, they were missing! He said he just wanted to understand my relationship with them better so he could understand why I'd hurt those those kids. But I knew better. Dr Fanshaw was not what he seemed. He was after my parents and – given that he wouldn't tell me what he wanted with them – it was pretty clear he intended them ill.

My parents had chosen to disappear, and *someone was after them*. Then the disguises they'd always worn suddenly made sense too. They'd spent all their time together living in hiding! From whom exactly? Perhaps *both* heaven and hell. Perhaps mixing simply wasn't allowed. Theirs was a forbidden love maybe.

I wasn't about to tell Dr Fanshaw anything. I played it innocent. But it became harder and harder to keep up the act – he started to ask me about my *feelings*, of all things, and I had to answer him fairly directly so that it wouldn't look like I was hiding something. He was clever like that, getting me to reveal things. It got so that I was running out of things to tell him. Soon I'd have nothing left but the truth. He tried to make me resent them, telling me that they'd gone off and abandoned me, that he wasn't sure they actually loved me. I was right on the point of declaring they would have left signs and clues for me to follow so that I could go join them. Right on the edge. It was then I knew I'd have to break out of the special unit, before I gave everything away.

Breaking out was easy. Some would call it magic, but it's more of a trick. There's no great mystery to it. My mum explained it to me once. If you're doing something that you don't want people to see, even if it's right in front of them, just tell them you're doing exactly what they want and expect you to do. 'I'm staying right here,' I told the nurse. She nodded as I walked straight out the door. Funny how such things work. Try it some time, if you're in a special unit, stuck with someone you don't like, or whatever. By the time they realise, you'll already be away.

I got home as quick as I could. I knew it was the first place the goons would come looking for me. I would have precious little time to find the sign or clue my parents had left for me. In something of a panic, I ran straight for the desk in my room, to get my old Nokia phone – Dr Fanshaw had taken away my iphone my first day in the unit. I'd get the old phone charged and simply call mum and dad! Idiot. They'd have ditched their phones, to avoid being tracked. Mum said some demons can literally pluck phone calls out of the air too. What to do? What? I went through the apartment looking for anything out of place. Anything. The lounge. The bathroom. Again the lounge. The kitchen. And there it was – on the fridge door. A photo of the three of us. It hadn't been there before. It was a close up, so it was impossible for anyone to know where it had been taken. I knew though.

I stuffed some clothes and snacks from the fridge into a rucksack and hightailed it out of there. The street outside seemed quiet – nothing but a man in a brown coat leafing through a magazine at the newspaper stand. I kept my eyes on him, but he never looked my way. There were no reflections for him to be looking in, and there were no suspicious-looking vehicles waiting nearby. And he couldn't have been a demon – I wouldn't have seen him in the first place if he had been.

Evading cctv as best as I could, I got across town to the café where the photo had been taken. There was no sign of anyone following me, and the hairs on the back of my neck didn't rise at any point. (Why *do* people always tell themselves they're imagining things when the hairs on their necks rise? Dad wasn't entirely sure, but he said it was probably to do with our living in *a less religious age*.) The sun was out, but the outside tables and chairs were empty. I stepped inside and was disappointed to find things just as quiet. Mum and dad weren't here. Deflated, I sank into a ludicrously comfy chair. How many days had I been in the unit? Did I really think my parents would have sat here waiting all that time?

'What'll it be?' the waitress asked me brightly. She was pretty, if you didn't mind slightly boss eyes, and not much older than me. She wore an overly-patterned top that would give you a headache if you looked at it too long.

'Er . . . I . . . have you seen any angels or demons in here recently?'

She had a laugh that was fragile like glass. 'Oh, we get them in here all the time.'

'You do?'

'Uhuh. You've gotta watch the demons though, cos they'll try and leave without paying. I think it's a matter of principle with them. Don't you think?'

'Um. I guess.'

'Still, it's odd to have demons with principles. Paradoxical even. Contrary buggers.' She shrugged. 'So?' She brandished her notepad, and waved her pen in the air like a magic wand.

'I'll have a coke, please . . . erm, Rachel.' (I'd read her name badge.) I smiled.

She leaned over me. 'Not going to run out on me without paying, are you?' She bared unusually sharp teeth at me.

'N-no. Here! I'll pay upfront.'

She took my coins – 'I'll bring your change' – and was gone.

The bell above the door rang and I turned to see a man in a brown coat enter. A brown coat! His face was turned away from me.

'Here. Your coke and your change.'

'K-keep it,' I replied.

'Here,' Rachel insisted. 'Take it. And your receipt. You'll need it. It gives you ten percent off your next visit. Here!'

I'd risen, picked up my rucksack and was edging towards the door, waiting to see which way brown coat would turn, so I could slip round the back of him. I put out a hand behind me, grabbed what Rachel put in my hand, and shoved it all in my pocket.

'You will come back, *won't* you, Astor?'

'Sure, sure,' I mumbled, saw my chance and flew out of there.

There were brown coats everywhere. And it wasn't just my imagination. On the stairs down to the underground. I u-turned, sprang back up and met another brown coat a dozen yards away. I swerved and took off down the road and into a market. Brown coats behind stalls shouting as soon as I came near. Brown coats perusing the stalls and turning at the raised voices. A cut left into an anonymous pub, where there were old men sitting alone in brown raincoats. Through there onto a parallel street, a backstreet. A moment of silence, with no one else there. My panting. And then someone stepping into the entrance of the alley. It was a dead-end. And a brown coat with collar turned up walking straight for me. I was trapped.

'Finished?' asked the big man casually.

'What?'

His eyes flashed. 'You didn't really think you could get away, did you?'

'What are you talking about?'

'Come on, Astor. Given I know who you are, what's the point of playing it innocent? Look around you.' He put his arms out wide and turned left and right. 'There's no one else here. So just who is it you are deceiving in all this? It's certainly not me.' His eyes became cunning. 'It must be yourself. It can only be yourself.'

'What do you mean? Let me go!'

'You can't escape. Surely you've already seen that. And deep down you know *why* you can't escape, don't you?' I shook my head in confusion. 'Come on, Astor. Enough with the denial. You've seen it for yourself. You can't escape what you already know. You can't escape the truth. It traps you. No matter how much you run from it, resist it and deny it, you still *know* it.'

'No.'

'You can't run from yourself. You can't escape yourself and your own mind. You'll never find them, you know. You can't. Because none of this real. If you think hard – think logically – you'll see none of it can be. Haven't you noticed how weird, surreal and impossible all this is? You've made up this fantasy for yourself. Think hard and you'll remember what's really happened to your parents.'

I backed away from him. 'No. No!'

The man showed understanding now. A helpless gesture of the hand as he came forward. 'Astor. Just think. Come back to the secure unit, where at least you'll be safe, where you won't be able to do any more harm to yourself or others with this delusion. Don't let it grow and overwhelm you. Let Dr Fanshaw help you with what happened to your parents.'

I looked around frantically now. There had to be some way out. 'Stop saying that!'

'Stop saying what, Astor?'

'Stop speaking as if . . . as if something bad happened to . . .'

'Happened to who, Astor? Your parents?' His voice dropped to a whisper: 'I'm sorry. About how they died in the car crash.'

'Liar!' I leapt forward, catching him off-balance. I ducked low, and his reaching near hand dragged off my back, failing to get a proper grip.

'Run then!' he called after me. 'Astor, you'll find there's nowhere to go and no way out. We'll be waiting for you at the unit, to help you. Come to us when you're ready, Astor. But don't leave it too long!'

No. No. No! It wasn't something I could have forgotten. It was ridiculous.

Ridiculous. The brown coat had to be lying. Had to be. He wanted to keep me apart from my parents . . . because . . . Well, it didn't matter why. There were probably a dozen reasons. I just didn't know them yet.

I slumped down against the wall, behind a bottle bank, alone at last. I needed to clear my head. And catch my breath.

I just needed to make sense of things, to get a handle on them.

The brown coat was trying to convince me that I was mad, that I was delusional. He was trying to convince me that my parents were dead. But weren't people after my parents? Why would he encourage me to give up searching for them? Why wouldn't he encourage me to keep looking, and then follow me to them?'

I had no answers. I didn't know anyone who did either. And I had no idea where to find any, now Rachel's café had proven a dead-end.

I wasn't even sure there was anywhere I could go. I couldn't exactly live here behind the bottle bank – even the secure unit, with its three square meals a day, would be better. Yet there didn't seem much alternative.

With a sigh I reached into my pocket to see how much money I had. A piece of paper fluttered free, the receipt from the café. There was writing on the back: *The Palace Picturehouse, 7pm x.* It was from Rachel! Surely she would take me to my parents.

I stood waiting outside the old cinema. It being midweek, there was hardly anyone around. Even so, I felt exposed. A brown coat could come out of the dark at any moment.

'Hey, gorgeous!' called a voice right behind me. I jumped. As I turned, a tall and beautiful girl leaned in and kissed me on the lips.

I pulled back in alarm. It took me a moment to recognise her beneath the makeup. 'R-Rachel? Y-you look . . .' She was dressed for a night out. 'Nice.'

She smiled. 'Did you get the tickets?'

'Er . . . no. What movie—'

'Well there's only the one showing, silly. *The Monster from the Black Lagoon.* A classic. You haven't seen it, have you?'

'N-no.' Wait. This was all wrong. 'Have you seen my parents?'

'No. I haven't heard of that one. Is it new? Come on, let's go inside. We don't want to miss the start.'

She thought we were on a date. She didn't know anything about my folks. I wouldn't be able to find them now. I became light-headed. It felt like losing them all over again. I didn't move as she went up the stairs to the entrance. 'I don't think–'

'Oh, no. Don't go thinking you can back out on me now!' She marched down the steps, took me firmly by the arm and proceeded to haul me upwards. 'I've spent far too long getting ready for tonight. And you're damn well going to buy me some popcorn.'

She dragged me to the ticket office and then to seats D6 and D7 in the theatre. There wasn't a single other person there. Resigned to watching the film, I sat back in my seat to try and work out what I was going to do. If my parents really were . . . Maybe only Dr Fanshaw could help me now. There was no one else. I couldn't imagine life without mum and dad. Maybe that was what had made me sick. Had I really done those things to those kids at school?

'This way!' she urged, pulling me up.

'Where are we–'

'Quick.'

I had to hurry to keep up. I nearly missed my footing in the dark. 'Wait. Rachel!'

'Here, Astor. Through here.'

I was bundled out an emergency exit. We were back in the cool night air, standing in pitch-black shadow. There was the reek of rotting vegetables and urine.

'They'll have lost our trail for a bit,' Rachel whispered. 'The smell and dark should mask us, but keep your voice down. They have sharp ears.'

'Y-you mean the brown coats? Who are they? What do they want? Where are my parents?'

'The suppressors work to prevent mortals having true knowledge of angels and demons.'

'What? But why?'

'Don't be daft. If mortals knew for sure that heaven and hell existed, then there'd be no issue of faith anymore, no real exercising of free will, and no actual way to judge an individual. It would be a disaster for creation.'

'But my mum's a demon, and my dad's . . .' My throat tightened. 'What do the brown coats want to do to me? To us?'

She let out a slow breath. 'They'll try to convince you you're delusional, that everything you thought was real was just a fantasy. If that doesn't work . . .'

'If that doesn't work, what? Tell me. Please.'

She sighed. 'If that doesn't work, there's a magic they can use, but it's messy.'

'Messy?' I squeaked. 'Messy how?'

'They often end up wiping too much of a person's memory. The victim's left as a vegetable. You'll probably be resistant to that magic, though, what with your parents and all. Meaning they'll only have one other choice.'

'You mean they'll kill me?'

'Shh. Keep your voice down. And try to keep calm. Intense emotion draws them.'

'Try to stay calm?' I hissed.

'This probably isn't the greatest date you've ever had, I know, but you've got to try and pull yourself together. You'll need to be quick about it too. We haven't got long, and I still need to teach you to move invisibly, or so the suppressors can't see you at least. Ready?'

'Yes,' I seethed. 'Get on with it.'

We peered out from the exit to the alleyway where we were hiding. There was no one in sight, but there were deep shadows all along the street where any number of watchers might be lurking. I was finding it incredibly difficult to take all this in while keeping my mind blank in the way Rachel had instructed. She'd told me to try and separate my senses from my thoughts, as if solving two problems at once, like rubbing your stomach with the circular motions of one hand while patting the top of your head with your other, or reading a book at the same time as listening to someone on the phone, or opening the door when you've got your hands full. 'Practice is all it takes. It'll almost be an unconscious habit after a while.

A few moments later, she was softly saying: 'Okay. We'll step out and stroll casually down that way. Just shadows elongating as the moon rises. Or a breeze drifting and dancing. Water flowing along a natural course. You get the idea? Images that'll confuse them. Come on, take my hand and I'll guide you along while you concentrate.'

'One thing about this date – it's certainly not been dull.'

'Stop it. Concentrate. Trust me. We can't afford to get caught.'

I frowned. 'Right.'

'Don't force it, though. Easy and calm. And . . . here we go.'

I liked holding her hand. It was becoming distracting, though.

'Later,' she growled, letting go. 'You men, honestly. Concentrate, Astor.'

I tried not to smell her perfume. 'Where are we going?'

'Shh. Stop thinking about that.'

'Are you taking me to my parents?'

'Best if I don't tell you out loud right now.'

Why did I know a moment of misgiving? Rachel was only trying to help me. Because she liked me. Maybe that was what felt odd. And she was pretty. That made her liking me even stranger. 'How do you know my parents?'

'Shh. They're close,' she whispered, her lips all but touching my ear. 'I'll explain everything once you've mastered your thoughts and we've got some distance away.'

No, she couldn't be helping me because of liking me. She'd given me the instruction to meet her when we'd only exchanged a few words. It had to be something else. She had to know my parents – hadn't my parents guided me to the café, to Rachel, in the first place? She had to be doing them a favour.

We'd walked for what felt like over an hour, circling back and crisscrossing until I was all turned around. I hadn't seen anything I recognised in a good while. Hopefully anyone still able to read my thoughts would be utterly confused.

'I don't sense any of them nearby,' Rachel murmured. She turned to face me and smiled with relief. Her eyes filled my vision. 'Okay, you can relax, Astor. Let your guard down a bit.' Her lips quirked. 'Is that what you've secretly been thinking? I'm not that sort of girl, you know!'

I felt myself flush. 'Surely it's rude to read people's thoughts without their permission!'

'I wasn't actually reading them. I was just teasing.'

'Oh.'

'So you *were* thinking about me?'

'No.' Pause. 'Maybe.'

She took my hand and squeezed it. 'We'll go on a proper date once this is all over. I promise. For now, though, we'd better work on getting you to your folks. Listen, there's a way for you to find them yourself. You're *connected* to them. What direction does your gut tell you they're in?'

'My gut?'

'Yes, your gut. You know how people sense when someone they love has suddenly died? Like a premonition? Or when separated twins know if the other one is in trouble? That's because of the connection. So just relax and tell me which direction you *feel* they are in.'

'You just want me to guess?' I asked doubtfully.

'If you like. However you want to understand it. What does your instinct or intuition tell you? That way? Or that way? What's the universe telling you? Close your eyes if it helps.'

'Er . . . along here?'

'Great. Let's go.' She was off immediately, and I had to trot to keep up.

The further we went, the more impatient Rachel seemed to get.

Something was wrong, I knew, but whenever I tried to slow she pushed on all the faster, and her distracted manner meant none of my breathless questions got a proper answer. She was too busy sniffing the air.

Frustrated, I halted, my hands going to my hips. 'Well at least promise me, once this is done, you'll get me a banana milkshake like the one you served in the café!'

She turned back with a snarl, her eyes blazing. Then she remembered herself and deliberately calmed. 'Whatever you want, Astor.' Her curves became accentuated with yearning. The scent of her surrounded me, her movements saw the air caress me, and her panting was at my ear. I breathed her in and tasted her. Her eyes drank me.

I backed away, raising guards around my mind, to block out her love-spell. 'You're not Rachel.'

'Sweetie, what are you talking about?'

'There was no banana milkshake.'

She smiled smoothly. 'Of course not. Silly me. I wasn't paying attention. I'm trying to get you to your parents. You want to see them, don't you?'

'If I have a connection with them, then *they* can find *me*. Why haven't they, then? Because it's not safe. Because of you and the brown coats. Funny how the brown coats aren't around. They've backed off because I'm showing you the way to my parents. That's it, isn't it? You're working for them. What have you done to the *real* Rachel? Who are you? *What* are you?'

'Astor, listen to yourself. You're sounding paranoid. It's not surprising, with all you've been through. Everything you thought you knew is upside down.' Her eyes were mesmerising. 'But you'll never get through on your own. You have to trust someone. Didn't I get you away from the brown coats? Didn't I explain what was going on? Haven't I shown you magic? And . . .' She pouted. 'I thought you liked me. Don't you? Not even a little?'

'I . . . I . . .' My mind was empty. She was right. Then a familiar voice came into my mind and I was saying the words out loud. '*You replaced Rachel somewhere between the café and the picturehouse. You played out this charade to make me dependent on you and to make me trust you. You even tried to seduce me. It's how you people operate. You know as well as I do I would have worked out the magic eventually. Now tell me who you are! I INSIST!*'

The dual powers of father's unrelenting righteousness and mother's passionate revenge bore down on her. She could not defend herself against it. 'Filthy half-breed!' she howled, and her features sloughed off.

'Fanshaw!' I gasped, feeling sick.

The doctor hissed. 'You will desist. Lead us to your parents at once or you will never see Rachel again. I abjure you in the name of God!'

An invisible hand gripped my heart and my knees buckled. I cried out in agony. '*Don't . . . hurt . . . her!* I keened. '*How . . . can I . . . lead you . . . like this?*'

A moment longer and I was released. 'Get up! Go on ahead.'

I looked up at him. Unforgiving eyes, a curled lip of disapproval, nostrils flared in disgust and harsh lines of contempt. I smiled in answer. 'I don't think so.' My eyes looked past him.

His head whipped left and right as he realised there were others present. 'No!'

My mother clamped a hand on his left shoulder, my father grasped his right.

They chanted an incomprehensible word and Fanshaw shimmered, and then disappeared completely.

I stumbled to my mother and hugged her. My father put his arms around us. 'A family again.'

'Mum,' I gulped. 'There's something I have to tell you. There were these boys at school–'

She caressed my cheek. 'Your father's taken care of it. They'll be fine. They won't even remember it. Such things happen when our kind comes of age. We'll need to talk about your anger management later, though.'

'Oh! And they've got Rachel.'

'Don't worry. They won't hurt her. They're not allowed. It's one of the rules. Once they realise she's of no use to them anymore, they'll simply let her go. If you're careful, you'll be able to see her from time to time. Your father will need to talk to you about girls later, though.'

I flushed. 'But the brown coats want to kill me! And they're trying to get to you.'

She smiled gently. 'Did Fanshaw actually say they would kill you? Or is that what you inferred? The latter, I think. He allowed you to believe it so you would need him. Now that we've sorted out the issue at your school, Fanshaw will struggle to get the resources to take on both your father and me. The suppressors usually have far bigger priorities, like rogue demons, dissolute angels, crazed cults, sick sacrifices, and so forth. We'll no longer be a serious concern, *as long as you behave yourself!* Understand?'

'Yes, mum.'

'Good. Now let's go home. You've already missed enough school as it is.'

And those were our first dealings with Fanshaw.

The Knight, Death and the Devil

A J Dalton

THE DEVIL'S REALLY NOT SO BAD ONCE YOU GET TO KNOW HIM. AS LONG as you know the rules, and stick to them of course, then there's only so much he can get up to.

He squired for me for many years, and a very capable squire he was too. He never complained at brushing down Walter – my long-suffering and, to be honest, bad-tempered mount – or bashing the dings out of my armour, or even at washing my soiled linen. And he wasn't a bad cook either – a bit heavy on the spices sometimes, but usually quite palatable.

The trick, you see, is to ignore everything he says, as if he weren't there at all, as if he were simply invisible and just a stray voice in the head. Certainly, very few others ever seemed to notice that he rode at my side, in my shadow, on the skeletal remains of a steed. The human mind only sees what it believes, you know, so it's of continuing astonishment that so few people actually believe in him.

And that's probably the way he prefers it. It means he can go about his mischief unobserved. He can brazenly walk up to a man, tweak him by the nose and whistle as if it were merely the wind at play. Or he will tap you on the shoulder, only for you to turn and find no one there. And then you feel another tap. Or he will sit right next to you, leering and playing with himself, when you're naked and going about your toilet of a morning.

But the trick is to ignore him. That way, none of his suggestions can seduce you. His talk of wealth, lusty fulfilment, revenge, a long-lasting life or good intentions must remain just that – as talk. You should never hesitate or give his words attention. You should always beware any new idea that occurs to you, as he may have tainted your thoughts, yet at the same time it is important not to start mistrusting your own mind. For that way madness lies.

Mistrust your own mind and you will find yourself pausing as you are about to deliver the killing stroke in the heat of battle. And that pause can prove fatal and costly. You must proceed as per your training and the commands of your King, for that will see you win safely through. Otherwise, Death will beat you to the punch and all will be undone. No more time to tip the scales of judgement in your soul's favour. No more time for heroic deeds, self-flagellation, prayer and penance. Death and the Devil are a pair of murderous thieves like that, looking to time their move perfectly. They'll have your soul from you and will be off into the night before you can even say. 'I repent!'

But do not be overly alarmed. Ignore him long enough and he'll get bored and wander off. One day, you'll wake up and he simply won't be there anymore. You may feel something tweak your nose, but it'll only be the wind at play. You may feel something tap you on the shoulder, but do not be concerned by it. Simply decline to turn around.

As I said, he's really not so bad once you get to know him.

Interview with the Angel

A J Dalton

[Transcript of a sound recording found in an abandoned office in Muswell Hill, London, UK]

First speaker: So how long have you been an angel?

Second speaker: Well . . . forever.

1st: Then . . . you were born when?

2nd: I wasn't. I have always existed.

1st: Okay. I see. So how does a person become an angel?

2nd: They don't.

1st: But–

2nd: Look, it doesn't work like that. Mortals do not *become* angels. Angels are angels.

1st: That hardly seems fair.

2nd: Fair isn't a 'thing'. Your statement is meaningless.

1st: I just don't understand why some people get to be an angel and others don't.

2nd: *No* people *get* to be an angel. Didn't you listen to what I just said? Maybe this was a bad idea after all. I feared you wouldn't be able to understand a word I said. Or you'd get it all back to front like your prophets did with the Bible and—

1st: No, no. It's being recorded. I won't get anything wrong. I promised you. Look, I just started things off on the wrong foot. Let me ask you a different question. Once we properly get into it – establish the right terms of reference and all that – then it'll be much easier. You'll see.

2nd: [*A pause*] Alright. Ask your question.

1st: Okay. Hmm. So what does an angel do? It isn't all sitting on clouds and strumming lyres, I imagine. Right?

2nd: [*Sigh*] Right. This is why I'm giving you this interview. It's time to correct some of the backward ideas you mortals have about angels. You have misunderstood, embroidered, manufactured and accrued so much that you have created a fantasy or mythology you believe in so much that it is delusional. It bears no resemblance to what is real. It blinds you to the nature of God's creation and its purpose. It blinds you to God Himself, to the true guidance and attempts to help you of His angels and to the insidious ways of those who are . . . less helpful, let's say.

1st: Oookay. There's a lot there. Can you give us an example of some of these things you say we've misunderstood or invented? You're saying angels don't play lyres?

2nd: Forget about the lyres. We play them no more or less than mortals. I'm talking about bigger things than that.

1st: What then? You all have wings, right? It must be great to fly everywhere. Though you won't be able to collect air miles that way . . . not that . . . angels would have much use for . . . Sorry.

2nd: It's always about the wings with you people. We don't have them.

1st: What? But you're wearing some now. What are you talking about?

2nd: Look, they're just how you perceive us. They're not literal. They're a visual metaphor of sorts. Creation is all one, so we can be in any part of it in the instant. Instinctively you mortals understand that creation, being a part of it, so you perceive us as having the spiritual means to travel as we wish. But we do not have wings. Okay?

1st: I guess. And they'd be a bit impractical.

2nd: What would?

1st: Wings.

2nd: I've already said – we don't have wings.

1st: Because they'd get stuck coming through doors, and you'd sit on them . . . not that you would . . . because you don't have any. Sorry. So! No lyres to speak of, and no wings. What else? Where's your halo? You do have one, right? Or have you misplaced it?

2nd: [*Pause*] Listen. Can we just drop the obvious stuff? Forget about cosmetic lyres, wings and haloes, yeah? Think about the bigger issues. I said you mortals were blind to the nature of God's creation and its purpose. Why don't you ask me about that? I said you were blind to God Himself, to the efforts and guidance of His angels and to the machinations of those set against us. Surely there's something you want to ask me there.

1st: Er . . . sure. What's the purpose then?

2nd: To test you mortals, so that you might learn, grow and improve. As long as you remain blind to that though, you'll never learn. You'll just 'bimble' along enjoying yourselves while remaining careless of consequence and self-improvement.

1st: Why improve?

2nd: What?

1st: Why bother improving? Is there some special reward for improving?

2nd: True communion with God, of course, once you have proven yourselves worthy.

1st: And what's so great about that?

2nd: Are you crazy? It's not something I need to *sell* to you.

1st: Well, that's just it, isn't it? 'Communion with God'? What does that even mean? It's very vague. Hardly very motivating.

2nd: I don't believe this. Surely you desire the wonder and glory of sharing yourself with God.

1st: Can't say that I'm all that bothered in truth. Quite happy as I am.

2nd: Intolerable ego!

1st: Why intolerable? That's what this whole free will shtick is all about, isn't it?

2nd: No. It is not.

1st: I think you'll find it is.

2nd: Well, yes. But it is not intended for you to demand God be answerable to you. That is blasphemy, sin and self-damnation.

1st: Have it your own way. Toe the party line, etcetera. I'm just saying that I – and many other like me, I imagine, have my *own* aims and desires in life. It's not for you or anyone else to tell me otherwise, is it? If He were to demand otherwise then there'd be no free will, he'd be a tyrant and I really wouldn't want anything to do with Him. And yet you, as His servant and voice, are telling me I *have* to aspire to this woolly communion you talk about, that I should define my life by it and enslave myself to it.

2nd: I'm not saying you *have* to do anything.

1st: Really? That's not how it sounded to me.

2nd: I was simply trying to encourage you . . . to help . . . Why are you mortals *like this*? You are so frustrating and contrary. Don't you want to improve yourself and ensure that your soul is saved beyond death?

1st: Why should it be lost or damned just because I live in terms of my own aims and desires? Again – and I come back to this – it hardly seems very fair.

2nd: It's not a democracy! It's not about equal opps and diversity. You don't get to *vote* on whether you get saved or not. God is not *elected* by you mortals, for crying out loud! It's not about 'fairness'. It's about virtue, sin, *your* behaviour, redemption, damnation and *accountability*. The only 'fairness' is the will of God. Salvation is communion with God, damnation is being denied Him. That's it. The end. Finito. If you knowingly *choose* not to seek communion with Him, then on your own head – on your own soul! – be it. See how you like it in hell.

1st: Is that a threat?

2nd: What?

1st: It's do-as-I-say-or-go-to-hell, is it?

2nd: Pretty much.

1st: I see. Hell is real then? Have you seen it? Have you *been there*?

2nd: No, I haven't been there, but–

1st: So how do you know it's so bad? Could just be heavenly propaganda, couldn't it?

2nd: [*Pause*] Are you seriously suggesting that the Bible and the word of God are mere propaganda? Is there no blasphemy from which you mortals will shy?

1st: You were going to tell me about hell? Or would you like to admit here and now that you really don't know much about it and that I might be better off interviewing some demon or other?

2nd: Mortal, why are you so adversarial? I am trying to tell you things that can help you and all your kind, and yet you refuse to hear it or allow it. Are you truly so hellbent on your own damnation? Or it is some sort of madness, for I cannot otherwise understand your obstinacy, obduracy and wilfulness.

1st: *Me* adversarial? You said it wasn't a democracy. You said it wasn't a matter of fairness. So I have to look after myself, then. I have to take it personally. There's no other choice. I *have* to be adversarial. Don't I?

2nd: Perhaps we can come at this from another direction. Why don't we start afresh, with some new questions?

1st: Perhaps, although some listeners will wonder if you're actually ducking the questions and issues just raised.

2nd: [*A sigh*] There's nothing I can do about those who are so cynical. In any event, they are likely to think this recording is actually a fake.

1st: Then why bother with this interview at all, if you're only preaching to the converted?

2nd: Because I have to try. Perhaps this interview will make just one atheist doubt themselves. If it helps save just one soul, then it's all worth it. Besides, I may not provide incontrovertible proof of the existence of angels and God, as otherwise that would remove the need for faith, the testing of mortals, the need for virtue and free will itself.

1st: Ah. But it'll be more than just this recording, won't it? There will be my testimony that I actually met an angel. There will be my articles. And you'll agree to a photo or two. Right?

[Long pause]

1st: Right? . . . Say something. What? No photos? Okay . . . Or articles? Sheesh . . . What about my testimony? I *am* walking away from this interview, right? Say something, damn you!

2nd: I'm sorry.

1st: What *do you mean* you're sorry? This wasn't part of the deal.

2nd: Do you have any other questions?

1st: What? Why? Why now? Why?

2nd: Ah, that old one. It's simply time, I'm afraid. It has to happen some time, after all.

1st: Why me? Why me?

2nd: Also a classic. I think we've kind of covered that already, haven't we? We're just going over old territory. Are you ready?

1st: No! No! What about the questions you haven't properly answered? What's hell like?

2nd: I've never been there, or within it more precisely, so I'm not entirely sure. But let's just say I doubt you'll enjoy it very much.

1st: What?! I'm not going there.

2nd: I will deliver you to its gates. You can ask your questions of the demons when I hand you over.

1st: No, you can't! I'm not ready. I have other questions. I repent. Yes! I repent.

2nd: I'm afraid it's too late for that. You have had proof incontrovertible of the existence of angels and God. Judgement has been passed.

1st: You bastard!

2nd: It is not I who is damned. I pity you, mortal, truly I do.

1st: No! Noo!

[Recording ends]

The Watcher

Sammy H.K Smith

As I packed away the charcoal and pencils, and wiped my blackened fingers on my jeans, it began to rain. Not the usual spitting, drizzly and slanting rain that I had grown to love whilst in England, but huge fat droplets that splattered and soaked through my tee-shirt in seconds.

'Fuck's sake,' I muttered, running into the church and dragging my rat-tailed black hair into a ponytail. 'Fucking weather.' I shook my jacket, soddening the pamphlets that lined the wall.

There was a deep rumble, followed by a crack of lightning that lit up the antechamber. I waited for at least fifteen minutes before giving in and calling for a taxi to the train station.

'Cassie, you're late. Where have you been?' Sheena asked, her big brown eyes full of interest as they flicked to my portfolio folder and up again. I sat down in the train carriage and opened a can of cider, gulping down the sweet apple and licking my lips. 'Did you finish?'

Nodding, I pushed the black folder across the table towards her. 'Have a look if you want. It's done. Hallelujah.'

She pulled me close and pressed her warm lips against mine. It was a ritual of late. Every time we were apart she would great me with a kiss and I would reply with a smile, unsure what to say. She had taken to introducing me as her girlfriend. I liked that she was happy, and girlfriend had a nice ring to it; it felt like a warm, safe cuddle.

'It looks incredible.' She lightly ran her fingers across the images, one by one. 'I can't believe how good you are.'

'Years of practise.' I grinned at her, raising an eyebrow as I finished the can and crushed it. 'I've been drawing for as long as I can remember.'

As the train hurtled through the villages and back towards London, I flicked through my sketches whilst Sheena leaned against my arm and slept. I took out my watercolour pencils and sketched the woman in the far left booth, watching her animated face as she talked to her friends. This would be the start of a new collection on human nature and emotion. The energy and drive hummed and buzzed as the colours flew onto the paper.

* * *

MY HEAD SNAPPED forward and my pencils went flying. A sharp lash of pain down my neck and back momentarily blurred my vision. The lights flickered a warm blue and a hum of electricity crackled in the ceiling. Sheena head-butted the table and there was a crunching and creaking of metal on metal that pierced through the metal-tanged air. So much screaming and crying, but there was a staccato wailing assailing me. Warm wetness trickled down my head to my ear. Touching my scalp my fingers came away bloody. Sheena groaned as I pulled myself up and fell into the gangway, tripping over cases and bags. The overhead baggage compartment hung twisted and torn from the carriage. The scream cut through me again, louder than the rest, throbbing at my ears and tearing at the pit of my stomach. Phones started to ring.

Sheena called for me, but I didn't turn back. The screams, the phones, the noise, all of it, was too much. Prising open the carriage doors I climbed over another bag and the acrid stench of the toilets made my eyes water. I stumbled into the corridor, wondering at first why I couldn't walk straight. The floor was tilted and after a few seconds the realisation that the carriage was twisted and on its side hit me. Looking out the smashed door window, I reached out and touched the tree leaf that poked through.

'Help me.'

He was wedged and propped up in the corner of the carriage; head twisted and almost resting on his shoulder. A gnarled and snapped branch speared his right thigh and hip. His blue jeans were nearly black and the blood slowly seeped into a puddle by his side. I stood, staring. My injured head was pounding.

'Help me, please,' he repeated.

I stared at the man, then the branch, then the wound and back to the branch again. My thoughts were like porridge, gloopy and thick. I couldn't move. I knew I needed to help but, in that moment, I didn't know what to do.

'Here, let me.' Hands grabbed my arms and firmly pushed me to one side. The man who had been sitting opposite us, Sheena and me, knelt down and shrugged off his suit jacket, pressing it against the branch. 'Keep the pressure on. What's your name?'

'Danny . . . McVeigh'. His voice shook. 'Thank you.'

'Can you help him?' The stranger indicated the jacket and, nodding, I knelt and held the jacket in place against the wound. The blood smelt sweet like cherries. I was still nodding. I couldn't stop.

'Ok, Danny. This lady will hold this for you. It'll be all right.' The man put a warm hand on my shoulder. 'What's your name?'

Mind blank, I stared up at him. He was in his forties, with wavy brown hair and blue eyes. He looked a little like Han Solo. I smiled. He furrowed his brow. Yes. Name.

'Cassie.'

'Great. Cassie, can you keep talking to Danny?' He squeezed my shoulder and something clicked inside, flooding me with warmth and heat. Danny groaned a little. His eyes were closed, his face was pale and his lips were a washed-out shade of pink. Touching his face, it was clammy and cold.

'Danny?'

He murmured an acknowledgement. The warmth continued to spread through me and my head and back burned. Han Solo was on his phone to the emergency services. I heard him mention the significant blood loss and serious injury, but I had to block his voice out because I was still struggling with my own thoughts.

'Danny, do you need me to call anyone?'

He made the tiniest of head movements, *no*. I continued to talk to him. I told him about my art and my trip around the country. I mentioned Sheena and panic burst through me as I realised I had left her. The memory of her head hitting the table flashed in front of me. Sickness churned in my stomach. Instinctively, I went to stand, but stopped. My hand was sticky with blood and I couldn't stop applying pressure to the wound. Head throbbing again, I hunkered back down.

'Services will be here soon.' Han crouched next to us. 'You can go to her if you want. I'll take over.' He placed a hand over mine. 'It's ok.' His blue eyes were warm and full of life. I glanced at Danny, his own eyes closed and lids flickering. I needed to stay. I couldn't get up and leave him, not now.

'No, it's all right.'

Just moments after Michael – Han Solo – had offered to take over, Danny gurgled and gasped, his body tensing, then flailing in spasms. Michael spoke quietly and with authority. *I was not to stop applying pressure. Don't look at Danny. Concentrate on his voice.* I did look. I had to witness it. Danny's eyes rolled back and his back arched. His face contorted momentarily before relaxing and his eyes rolling forward. He stared ahead, not focused on anything, and exhaled. His mouth remained open. As did his eyes.

The warmth left me, replaced with emptiness and the cold. I sat there with him until the emergency services arrived. He couldn't be alone, it wasn't right. Michael stayed with me, re-assuring me that I couldn't have done anything more for him. That Danny was in a better place now. I never liked the phrase 'hollow words', for words aren't hollow if they are said with the best of intentions. Michael was kind and comforting, but his words did nothing to assuage the despair. Danny was gone. His life had been snatched cruelly from him, and I had watched it happen.

* * *

'DANNY MCVEIGH, HEIR to McVeigh Enterprises, dies, aged 33'.

I held the newspaper clipping in my hand. It was the first anniversary of his death. Danny's smiling face stared at the camera as he posed with two supermodels outside a restaurant in London. I hadn't recognised him that day on the train, but he had been a playboy of sorts. Son of a media mogul and yet a philanthropist, he was one of the 'good guys'. The public mourned his death, but I had witnessed it.

'Aren't you going to say anything?'

Sheena's accusing voice broke into my reminiscence, and looking up from the paper snippet I saw she stood in the doorway with two large suitcases to either side of her. Her dreadlocks were scraped into a bun and her thick rimmed glasses perched at the bottom of her nose. I shook my head.

She opened her mouth and then closed it. She was always pushing a little deeper, asking a few more questions each time, but I wasn't ready to share with her. She knew I was alone and that my father had wanted me to travel the world and get to know more people, but I didn't talk about him often. We weren't that close anymore. His work and his people took up all of his time and energy. I didn't want to talk to her about it, about any of it.

'You've changed, Cassie. Since that day on the train, you've changed. You're colder than a fish.' No longer did she sound angry or upset when discussing the accident. Instead she was resigned and . . . tired. She closed the door behind her and struggled down the steps to the waiting taxi. I ashamedly felt a sense of relief. She hadn't been happy these last six months and all I wanted was her happiness. When she had told me she no longer loved me, I understood, even though the pain and emptiness hurt more than I thought possible. During our last argument I had pushed out the words 'I love you', but the disbelief on her face at my protestation was enough to silence me. I knew then that it was too late. I hadn't given her enough of myself. She wanted more and I couldn't let go. I couldn't give her everything.

As her taxi pulled away, I made the decision to move away from the miserable city of London.

* * *

It was three years later that I met Helena in a coffee shop in Oxford. I had moved, as intended, and started working in a small and alternative clothes shop in the centre of Oxford city during the day and taken on part time hours cleaning at the hospital in the evenings. It meant my weekends were free for socialising and working on my art.

That December morning, whilst sipping my coffee and mentally prepping myself for another day with my overly talkative manager, my routine was broken by the sound of pure happiness. Looking up, I watched her laughing with friends as she ordered a coffee, then deliberated over a cake and finally ordered two. I was unable to stop the smile spreading across my face as she then recalled a joke and burst into giggles before the punchline. Looking over and making eye contact with me, her giggles continued and my smile grew. She looked away first, directing her friends over to a table just a few feet away and sat with her back to me. Her blonde hair was loose and long. It took me a few seconds before I went back to reading the newspaper. I didn't want to appear like a weirdo, watching her from afar.

'You've been reading that page for about five minutes. Is it interesting?'

Looking up, she leant over my table and tapped her thin fingers on the paper. She bit her nails, and even the light pink polish couldn't hide the ragged tips.

I took a sip of coffee, stalling for time and a witty reply, but none came. 'It's an interesting article,' I finally replied, hating that I sounded so standoffish.

Unbidden, she sat down and my stomach swirled with excitement and nerves. As she raised an eyebrow and grinned, I seized the opportunity. 'I'm Cassie.'

'Helena.'

It was the start of something special, I knew it.

* * *

I missed work and she skipped her lectures. Together we walked around Christchurch gardens and admired the colourful Christmas lights and displays. I paid no attention to anyone else, though. I told her about my father and his wish for me to experience independence, although he didn't bother to talk to me anymore, and I told her that I'd never known my mother and how I envied those who had grown up with the love of two parents. It was unnerving how easily the words spilt from my lips. I touched lightly on my past relationships and the incident on the train, glossing over witnessing the death of Danny McVeigh and instead focusing on the aftermath. Instead of the usual sympathetic nods and comments that so many others afforded me, she remained quiet and just listened. It was reassuring and relaxing.

Throughout the day I kept replaying the image of me holding her hand in my mind. I would gently slip off my gloves and interlock our fingers in a seamless motion, but every time I went to do so, something interrupted me just as I had built up the courage. A cyclist would speed through the park singing carols, or sirens from the nearby police station would make us jump, or, even worse, our phones would go off and we would make awkward excuses to our friends and bosses as to why we couldn't see them. I wondered if fate or God was intervening but quelled the childish thought.

That afternoon, after I'd spilt my heart and the story of my life, she told me about herself. Helena was gregarious and open, and the eldest of six children. Her parents were divorced but she held together the relationships of her siblings with the authority and stubbornness afforded to the eldest child. In her final year at Oxford Brookes University, she was studying Computer Programming and hoped to move to the seaside and design computer games. She hated being landlocked and yearned to be near the sea.

By 4pm it was dark, and I knew that she would soon be leaving to attend a party at a friend's. As we wandered slowly to the gates of the gardens, her fingers slipped between my gloved ones and squeezed gently.

'Wanted to do that all day. Didn't know if it would be weird,' she blurted out. I think she blushed but the cold had bitten her face, and her nose, cheeks and ears were already red. 'Can't believe we've been talking all day. It feels like I've known you forever.'

I seized the opportunity under the mistletoe of the gates. Pulling her closer I leant down a little and we kissed. Although her skin was cold and her lips chapped, she was warm and everything I desired. She kissed me back and I smiled as she tiptoed to reach up. My heart ached. The pain of what felt like an eternity of depression and despair started to slip away and, as I broke from our embrace and saw her lick her lips a little and smile back at me, hope blossomed. She gave me her number and I walked her to the bus stop, still holding her hand. She suggested we meet the next day at the covered market for coffee and present shopping. I agreed immediately, then berated myself for being overly keen. As sharp as a hawk, Helena laughed as she got on the bus and turned to me. 'Don't worry. I do this to all the girls,' she said with a flirtatious lilt in her voice. 'Ok, that's bullshit. I'm a virgin,' she added, laughing in wide-eyed shock at her unsolicited confession.

I didn't get a chance to reply. She skipped down to the back and sat down. As the bus pulled away, we waved to one another through the rear window.

* * *

WE MARRIED EXACTLY six months later at the Bandstand in Brighton. It pissed it down. The rain bounced off the stony beach with obnoxious forthrightness. Helena had graduated with a respectable 2:1 and been offered a job at a small design company and I keenly followed. I had no job placement waiting for me, but it didn't matter. Since our first meeting we had never spent a day without speaking. On Christmas Day, some twenty days after Christchurch, we video chatted for two hours and through her phone camera I met her siblings and her mother. Laying on my bed in my room, eating my microwave dinner, I could see where Helena inherited her beauty and bolshiness. Her mother, Robyn, was a formidable woman and, after our cursory introductions, she moved straight on to grilling me about my intentions for her eldest. It was Stephen, the youngest son, who saved me by pouring Robyn a glass of red wine and distracting her. Helena found it most entertaining.

She proposed on Valentine's Day, apologising for the tackiness of it whilst sliding the Haribo ring on my finger and proclaiming me as hers and she as mine. Never had I seen a more beautiful person than my fiancée that day. Never had I experienced such bliss. We planned with speed, ignoring friends and family who chanted 'marry in haste, repent at leisure'. We were in love. I took her name. My father hadn't even acknowledged my message about the wedding.

* * *

ON OUR FIFTH wedding anniversary, we sat in the waiting room. The bright florescent lights accentuated every pore and flaw of our faces. Helena's eyes were wide, her gaze flitting from the floor, to the posters on the wall, to the pamphlets on the coffee table and back again. Her skin was waxy with the sheen of sickness and sweat. Her fingers were interlocked with mine. We didn't speak to one another. Not even with the doctor mentioned the words 'terminal' and 'Macmillan'. I found myself speaking for us both, my voice not quite my own. It was flat and unwavering, perhaps even a pitch lower than normal.

'Is there anything that can be done?'

He didn't answer my question, and instead spoke of trials and treatments to extend the inevitable. He wanted to make Helena comfortable and ensure she didn't suffer. I wanted to tear the tumour out of her, to rip open her stomach and cut it out, there and then. Knowing that my wife carried this disease and death inside of her filled me with fury. Under that fury was fear. It was only my anger that kept me calm. I couldn't let her see I was afraid, but I didn't want to let the anger be all that kept me going.

* * *

'CAN I GET you a cup of tea?'

Looking up from my magazine across to the hospital room door, an elderly hospital worker stood smiling at me, wringing her hands but waiting patiently for my reply. I shook my head. Helena lay sleeping, an IV drip in each arm, her curvaceous form eaten away by the cancer. The worker nodded and left.

'Mrs Evans, can I have a word?' Doctor Lloyd now stood in the doorway and beckoned me over. We walked down the hallway and into his office.

'It's nearly time,' he eventually said. 'Would you like to call anyone to say their goodbyes?'

I pulled out the list of names and numbers from my pocket, staring at my wife's cursive handwriting. The fear gone, the anger gone, I was empty and washed-out. It was time, again, to watch someone die. Not someone. My wife. My *wife*. My voice growled inside. The anger was back. Hot and cloying. I slammed the list on the doctor's desk and walked away, back to Helena's side. I wouldn't move now, not until the end. Why her? Why Helena? She was gentle and kind. She cried at pictures of otters holding hands, for fuck's sake. She would have been a great mother. Fuck you, God. Fuck you. Why her? The voice continued to growl and scream inside, prowling like a tiger, bouncing off my skull cage.

'You look tired.' Her voice was a whisper, each syllable a struggle. I held her hand in mine, ignoring the clamminess of her skin and quelling my thoughts. I needed to concentrate on her. On us, this last time, but the stench of impending death hovered around us, bitter and putrid, sweet and suffocating.

'I'm fine, babe.' I stroked her face, savouring the touch, memorising every fleck of green in her eyes and the freckles on her nose. 'I love you.'

'I love you more,' she replied. 'From . . . the moment . . . we met.' The pauses between her words were getting longer and her eyes were closed now. She fumbled for her drip, hitting the button and releasing another shot of morphine.

'Until I met you, I was empty. I had lived, but not truly. You welcomed me into your family and made me feel wanted. Feel like I had a chance to belong to someone, that I had a purpose in life other than just wandering around. My purpose was to love you.' I had practised that piece several times over the last few weeks. I wouldn't have a chance to say these words again.

She didn't reply straight away, and for a terrifying moment I thought she had left me. There was a slight squeeze of my hand and she forced out, 'I'm scared, Cassie.'

Tears fell. I couldn't hold them anymore. This was real and there was nothing I could do. *Please, God. Please. Don't take her from me.*

'Don't be scared, my love. I'm here. I'm never leaving you. Ever. I promise.' I wiped my eyes and then covered her face in soft gentle kisses. If she opened her eyes again, I didn't want her to see my sadness.

'Will . . . you . . . look after . . . Oscar for me?' She paused and exhaled.

Our cat. Our fucking cat. He would miss her so much. Every night he prowled the flat meowing for her, sniffing my clothes on my return and scratching at the door and searching the rooms. Every night when I broke down in tears, he would console me, rubbing his face against mine and curling into my side as I slept.

'Always.'

Silence. The blood beat in my chest and ears, my heart rate growing faster. She didn't move. No, no, no. The beep of the machine cried out for us both. Her death knell.

* * *

IT WAS COLD. My fingers curled and refused to open properly, stiff with inactivity. I lay on my side, hugging her final portrait close to my chest and not caring that it crumpled and creased while Oscar lay at my feet. The tears didn't stop. *Please God, no. Not her. Please. I'll do anything to have her back. I promise I'll go to church. I'll pray more often. I won't ask you for anything again. Just please, give her back to me. Please God. Please.* It didn't matter that she was already gone, her body cool and empty. I knew that. I knew she wasn't coming back but it didn't stop the ache deep inside for her to return. The blood pumped around my body, hot and burning. Anger bubbled at the unwelcome taunt that I was still breathing. That I was here and she was not.

I had seen death many times. I watched men grasp desperately for life on the battlefield of Banquan, the fear flooding their eyes and leaking down their faces as they realised the futility of prayer to their gods. I was there in the place you know as Troy when the fires ravaged the city and children screamed for their already slaughtered fathers. I soothed the victims of the plague in London as their skin blistered and their bodies festered from the inside out. Flanders, the Somme, Dunkirk, Afghanistan, Iraq, I watched and released tears as blood flowed freely and without care, but none of it caused as much pain as her final gasp of air and the slow exhalation of life. I loved them all, but I loved her the most. She was the Queen of my mortal heart and I had fulfilled my role in watching her die, honouring and yet dishonouring Him in equal measure.

Cassiel the Watcher, I am to watch only. Love in the human domain was too complicated, too painful and too deep. Father had warned us of such forbidden things, and so these tears of release I shed will be my last. Cassiel the Watcher, I am to watch only. Never will I love again.

The Lucky Ones

Michael Bowman

'MIRANDA, DID YOU SYNC YOUR DATA?'

'Mu-um!' Miranda whined from the kitchen. 'I'll be late for school!'

'Did you?' her mother asked again, sternly.

'No.'

'Do it now.'

'But . . .' Miranda began, then gave up as her mother's stare silenced all protest.

'What about you, Jerry?'

'Yes, dear, I'll do it right now,' Jerry purred, kissing his wife Vanessa on the cheek and winking at his daughter. He turned towards the front door, pausing by the full length mirror to check his tie was straight. A tall, thin black box was mounted on the wall beside the mirror. Across the top of the box was the word Lumecor in shiny, embossed letters, while within the box's shiny black surface glowed three red lights. Jerry could see his reflection in the blackness as he pressed the palm of his hand against it. Instantly, a green progress bar appeared in the surface above his fingertips and began slowly crawling from left to right. Glancing around while he waited, Jerry caught sight of the mirror in the corner of his eye. If he turned his head while straining his gaze as far over his shoulder as possible, he could make out a circle of bright white light glowing under the collar of his shirt at the base of his neck. It was an implant called a HALO, Hemispherical Allocortical Life logger and, like smart phones, almost everyone had one.

'Oh! Did I tell you about Adrian?' Vanessa said, coming up behind him as he stood with his hand on the box.

Jerry frowned. 'No. What about Adrian?'

'He died yesterday.'

'Really?' Jerry breathed. 'How?'

'Traffic accident. Some idiot in a BMW was texting and ran right into him.'

'Ouch.'

Vanessa shook her head. 'Apparently it was very quick. He was killed instantly.'

'Oh, that's good. When did you find out?'

'I was talking to Rachel, last night,' Vanessa replied, naming Adrian's widow.

'Was she alright?'

'Oh, yes. She just said how inconvenient it all was. They were supposed to go to dinner with her parents.' Vanessa laughed. 'Rachel said she bet Adrian did it on purpose . . . he hates having dinner with the inlaws!'

Jerry chuckled. He could imagine Rachel saying that. 'How did their kids take it?' he asked. Rachel and Adrian had two kids, five and seven.

'Oh, they were fine. Rachel explained it all and told them Dad would be back soon, and they went to bed like normal. Kids are so resilient.'

Jerry nodded in agreement. As he did so, the green progress bar reached its destination. He removed his hand from the shiny black surface and the light from his HALO implant dimmed and went out, leaving no trace of its existence beneath the skin of his neck.

'Miranda!' Vanessa called, again, walking back into the kitchen. 'Hurry up!'

'I'm coming!' Miranda replied as she swept tablet, ereader and headphones into the open end of her bag.

'Have you got your lunch?'

'I'll get dinners.'

'But I made you a lunch!'

'Mu-um! My bag's full!'

Meanwhile, Jerry had opened the front door and was standing on the step, waiting. He heard an electric whine and turned to see a blue and white Lumecor vehicle drive past. The boxy vehicle pulled up in front of a house a few doors down the street. The interior was hidden behind black, one-way glass but as the side door slid open, Jerry caught a glimpse of the luxurious upholstery which cradled its current occupant. The passenger stepped out just as the front door of the house was flung open and two excited children ran down the driveway. They leapt into the arms of the man who stood, blinking, in the sunlight. A woman followed, her face a beaming smile as she leant forward over the heads of the children to kiss him.

Miranda appeared at Jerry's elbow. 'Is that Adrian?' she asked. 'Is he back already?'

Jerry nodded, his smile mirroring Miranda's as they watched. Meanwhile, unnoticed by the happy reunion, the Lumecor vehicle had closed its door and was now discretely gliding away down the street.

'We'll be late,' Jerry muttered, glancing at his watch. 'Where is she?'

'Bye, Mum!' Miranda called as she burst between them and ran out the door. 'Come on, Dad!' she called over her shoulder. 'We'll be late!'

'Miranda! Did you...?' her mother began, but then noticed that there were now two little green lights glowing on the surface of the box. When had she done it? Vanessa wondered, watching the car drive away. Then she recalled something she'd seen on a TV documentary. Apparently, the younger you were the quicker you could sync your data. It was something to do with the plasticity of a child's brain.

Now, as she approached the box herself, she could see coloured text floating in the black surface. One word read 'Jerry' and the other 'Miranda' and both glowed green. The remaining text said 'Vanessa' and glowed red. And there was plenty of space for more. Some families were larger, but Jerry and Vanessa had only one child, and most mornings Vanessa felt that was more than enough! She sighed with exasperation as she pressed her own hand on the black plastic. Why did it always have to be such a drama? she thought as she watched the green progress bar slide from left to right. But as she stood back and regarded the three little green lights, she could not help but smile with satisfaction. Her family was safe for another day.

* * *

THEY SAT BY the curb opposite the school entrance. The engine purred while Jerry tapped his fingers on the wheel as he waited for Miranda to get her things together.

'Why do you always have to pull everything out of your bag, again?' he moaned.

'Da-ad, I lost my phone!'

'Have you found it?'

'Yes.'

Jerry glanced across at the school where the pupils were filing in through the doors. 'Miranda, you'll be late,' he said.

'Da-ad!'

'What?'

'I've lost my book!'

Jerry frowned. 'Book?'

'There it is!' Miranda exclaimed, retrieving it from the foot well. But before she could stuff it into her bag, Jerry plucked it from her grasp.

'Wow,' he breathed. 'I haven't seen this for a few years. Not since I used to read it to you when you were younger. Why have you brought it to school?'

'We're doing a project and we have to bring in our favourite books and talk about them,' Miranda explained.

'Really? And you chose this one?'

'Of course!'

Jerry raised his eyebrows in a curious expression. 'Oh? Why's that?'

'Well, because you used to read it to me,' she said, blushing slightly.

Jerry smiled and ruffled her hair. 'Treasure Island,' he said, reading the front cover, then flicked the pages open at random. Across the street the last few kids were already filing up the steps and into the school. 'Da-ad! I'm gonna be late!' Miranda complained and made a grab for the book.

But Dad was feeling playful. 'Arrr!' he growled, pretending to be a pirate. 'This 'ere be my treasure, so it be!'

'God, that's bad,' Miranda sneered. 'No one even says that in the book.'

Jerry pursed his lips. 'Well then, what do they say?' And he flicked through the pages.

'Da-ad! Miss is looking at me!' Miranda wailed, catching sight of her teacher standing on the steps. 'I'll get in trouble!'

'Aye! Because them that die'll be the lucky ones!' Jerry replied, quoting from the text.

Miranda reached across and snatched the book out of his hands. 'Thank you, Long John Silver,' she said with a giggle, then dove out of the car and hurried across the road.

Jerry watched her go, then smiled again. Treasure Island. That brought back memories. He glanced at the dashboard clock and clucked his tongue. He'd better get to work or he'd be late, too!

As if in answer to this thought, a Lumecor vehicle slid past him. Jerry pulled out and followed it all the way to its destination. Only after they had both passed through the gates of the Lumecor complex did they part ways: the van turning left into the depot where the driverless vehicles were serviced, while Jerry turned right for the staff car park, which was nestled in the shadow of the Lumecor main building. As he opened the car door and swung a leg out he paused, thinking once again of the happy reunion between Adrian and his family. He frowned as he pictured Adrian's face. Surely there was something they could do about that? Jerry thought, recalling the pale pink colour of the man's skin. Surely there was a way to restore people's sun tan as well as their natural pigmentation? He pursed his lips as an idea began to form and he nodded to himself. Yes. That might work, he thought as his shoes clicked along the pavement towards the main entrance. He'd send an email to the Director of Product Development first chance he got.

* * *

MIRANDA HAD ALWAYS liked school. Her parents were paying for her to attend a real one, rather than rely on the free home schooling service provided by the government; Jerry and Vanessa had not wanted their child educated by a big smiley face on a computer screen that spoke in monosyllables. Neither had they wanted her to sit exams that consisted of multiple choice questions on subjects like supermarket shelf-stacking, or how to sanitise a hotel room toilet. Jerry and Vanessa dreamt of a brighter future for their daughter.

But going to real school had its downsides. Things like expensive fees, the school run every morning and teenage boys. One boy in particular, called Karl, wouldn't leave Miranda alone. Every time she checked her messages there was one from Karl. Usually three or four from Karl. Most of them just said 'hi' or 'wat ya doin?'

hi
hi
hi
wat ya doin?

But now and then she'd get a weird one.

do u beleev in angels?

Miranda had worried about that one for a while. It was very stalker-ish. She never answered any of them. Karl was creepy. As she was fond of telling her friends, 'If it was just him and me at the end of the world, the human race would go extinct!' But at the same time she didn't want to antagonise him by blocking him because, as well as being creepy, his dad was some sort of manager at Lumecor, which probably made him her Dad's boss, and Miranda didn't want to take any chances. Even at the tender age of thirteen everyone at school knew who you could mess with, and who you couldn't. Not unless you wanted to find yourself at home all day in front of the big smiley face. Then one day Miranda had got another message from Karl. It was a picture of his genitals.

On that day Jerry and Vanessa had gone into school for a meeting with Karl's parents, the Head Teacher, a social worker and Karl. Miranda had waited in the classroom with her teacher, Miss Hendricks, to keep her company. Karl had been told to apologise, in writing, but this proved a great challenge for Karl, who had a hard time spelling words like 'apologise'. Miranda later learned that he had become very angry and frustrated over it. Then she found out that one of her frenemies had told Karl what Miranda had said about him and the extinction of the human race. Maybe that was why Karl sent her a picture of a gun.

After the second meeting Karl no longer attended real school and Miranda had got on with her life until that morning, when Jerry dropped her off on his way to work. As Jerry drove away, following the Lumecor van, Miranda felt her phone vibrate while she was halfway up the steps of the school.

'Miranda? Are you alright?' Miss Hendricks asked when she saw the girl's expression.

But Miranda didn't reply. She was still staring at her phone. It was a message from Karl. The first in months. It was brief and to the point.

I jst kild my parents. Ur next

Jerry's car was on two wheels as it rounded the corner and sped towards the school gates. There was no one waiting on the steps as he took them three at a time. The big doors remained firmly shut as he hammered on the bullet proof glass, gesturing wildly to the receptionist at the desk inside to press the button that would open them. But she just stared back, tight-lipped, a security guard standing behind her.

'I'm Miranda's father!' he yelled. 'I'm her father!'

Blue lights flashed at the far end of the street. Two cars approached, driving almost as fast as Jerry had been. He stopped banging on the glass and turned to look at them. He was breathing hard, like an athlete at the end of a race, but he told himself it was alright. Miranda was inside, protected by the bullet proof glass and the school's security guards. And now the police were here. It was going to be alright. She was going to be safe.

'Why can't we get in?' asked a voice behind him.

'It's a lock down,' Jerry replied, breathing heavily as he watched the approaching blue lights. 'There's some kid with a gun.'

'I know,' the voice growled with a pronounced adolescent twang. Jerry turned around and looked straight down the barrel.

'The angels say we all gotta die,' the voice grated. There was a click as the safety catch came off.

'Please,' Jerry said. 'Please, just don't hurt my d . . .'

A sound like a thousand teeth chattering all at once rattled in Jerry's ears. He looked into the boy's eyes and saw them bulge, saw the boy's face twist into a grimace, saw his lips peel back from his teeth like a dried out corpse. His whole body was trembling, which made the barrel of the gun shake violently. Then the chattering sound stopped and the boy collapsed, folding onto the ground like jelly. Now there was shouting. Jerry didn't hear the words. He felt numb. Even his vision was dissolving into a haze. His eyes remained fixed on the boy and, as he looked, he saw two lengths of thin wire attached to the boy's chest. The wires gleamed brightly in the sun. The boy moved a little. 'Yurr . . .' he slurred, trying to speak. 'You're killing them.'

Jerry found his voice. 'Killing who?' he whispered.

An angry, shouting man in blue entered the corner of Jerry's vision, pointing a boxy looking gun at the boy and screaming instructions. The blue man reached down and pulled the gun from the boy's limp fingers. Then a second blue man appeared and roughly grabbed the boy's body, flipping him over and pulling his limp arms behind his back. The boy's face was crushed into the pavement, his mouth smeared against the concrete, dribbling saliva like a slug trail. But Jerry could just make out his next words before his body was hoisted upright and he was dragged away.

'You're killing the angels.'

* * *

THAT SAME DAY the news carried a story about a teenager who had shot his parents dead over breakfast. He had been on his way to school to kill his girlfriend when he'd been arrested. Miranda was very upset about being described as Karl's girlfriend. Even as she sat with her parents, giving a statement to the police, her phone buzzed with updates as both her frenemies and Best Friends mocked her.

> Girlfriend? Freek!
> Did u shag karl? I bet u did
> U an karl deserv each other
> sycho b1tch

Oblivious to the effect their reports were having on one girl's life, the media continued their coverage with a news article under the headline: Judge says murder 'Not a crime'. There was a video of the judge's summation: 'No murder has been committed. The victims are alive and well and sitting in the court as I speak. Neither may the state pursue a charge of attempted murder as, clearly, murder has been rendered impossible through the victims' use of technology. At best, the state may pursue a prosecution based on common assault, for which the maximum tariff is three months detention in a young offenders' institution.'

The article was accompanied by a picture of Karl standing between his freshly restored parents. They bore expressions of sadness and disappointment on their brand new, untanned, unblemished faces as they gazed down at their sullen, slouching killer. Below was a caption which read: Murdered parents vow to stand by their son. A subheading added: Killer claims angels told him to do it.

One Year Ago . . .

THE MID-MORNING SUN slanted through the narrow, slit-like windows along the top of the high, white walls. Bright yellow robot cranes hung upside down from monorails that criss-crossed the roof like the map of the London Underground.

The void between the roof and the floor was filled with constant motion as each robot hoisted its load into the sunlit air, swung it across the building and then lowered it again. The scene resembled a giant game of Tetris in which the blocks floated up as well as down, and all of it happened in near total silence, with only a barely perceptible electronic hum.

The high walls were so tall that the sunlight could not reach the floor. Down there, the only light came from the harsh glare of thousands of white strip lights. They switched themselves on and off only as needed, so that a distant observer could track a person's progress across the floor by watching the slowly moving pool of light that followed them. Below the lights coiled a complex mass of pipes and valves and foil-wrapped conduits, all twisting and turning across the width of the building like a giant jungle gym. But even this was not the end of the journey, because below this plumber's nightmare sat the storage tanks: huge, heavy, sheer-sided and filled with thick, amber-coloured liquid, each one was individually bigger than a house, and there were thousands of them. Thousands, crowded together across the vast floor of the building.

The floor. Shiny, black and seamless, like the memory hubs that sat quietly in every home across the country. It ran in broad avenues east to west between the rows of honey-yellow tanks, and squeezed itself down narrow passages that ran north and south, separating each tank from its neighbour. These passages were so narrow that a grown man could not pass without his shoulders rubbing the glass on either side. Nor could he tilt his head far enough to see the top of one tank before the back of his skull hit the glass of the tank behind him. Only in the broad avenues was there space to look up and around; to gaze in wonder, and with a little fear, at the biggest enclosed space ever constructed by humanity.

They had levelled an entire city to find enough land to build this place, and done so gladly because within these walls, and many more like it, humanity was safeguarding its own future. Or so they thought.

* * *

'This is so cool!' said the gaunt-looking boy as he stared up and up and up, tilting his head back so far that he looked like he might fall over. The other kids in the school group started laughing. 'He thinks it's cool!' they sniggered. 'Geek!' they said, and shook their heads and rolled their eyes. The boy shrank under the weight of their disapproval, dropping his gaze as he drifted to the back of the group. Jerry watched this happen and sighed inwardly. Why did they have to do that? he wondered. At least Miranda hadn't joined in. There she was, near the front, her eyes scanning the tablet they'd each been given as part of the school open day at Lumecor. She was such a clever girl, and popular too! Jerry realised he was smiling with pride when he should be talking about the next stop on the tour.

'This,' he said loudly, 'is a storage tank.' He drew the group's attention with an exaggerated gesture that made his long, white lab coat swoosh like a cape. 'This tank is number zero four one seven slash b,' he added, squinting at the label. 'This is where we keep some of the human body templates until they're needed. Would anyone like a closer look?' he asked, stepping aside. Several children peered at the dense, honey-coloured liquid. 'I can't see anything,' a girl with a turned up nose whined.

'Why don't you come closer?' Jerry said. The girl stepped forward and squinted into the gloom. Suddenly, she squealed in fright and ran back into the group. 'There are people in it!'

At this, the whole group rushed forwards, pressing themselves against the glass. There were gasps and murmurs. Then the phones came out as everyone tried to get a picture of the skeletal human shapes that floated within. Human shapes, but not quite human. They floated in the thick, murky liquid with their legs together, arms outstretched and chins lowered until they were almost touching their chests. Each body was suspended by thousands of tiny, hair-like filaments that sprouted from the back of their necks, down their spines, and along the length of their arms. The filaments fanned out into the surrounding liquid as though blown on an invisible wind, before rising up and out of sight towards the plumber's nightmare of pipes and machinery at the top of the tank. Some of the children had pressed their foreheads against the glass and were trying to see to the bottom of the tank, but Jerry knew they couldn't. It was too deep, at least another hundred feet down below floor level and the nutrient matrix, the honey-coloured liquid, was too murky. All they would see was the shadowy suggestion of many more heads and shoulders hanging motionless in the amber abyss; an abyss that, Jerry knew, contained many hundreds more resting just out of sight. And this was just one storage tank. It was all very spooky, even for Jerry, who worked here every day.

'Are they alive?' turned-up nose asked.

'No, they're . . .'

'Why don't they have any skin?' asked another.

'Look! They don't have any lips or skin or anything! You can see all their teeth.'

'They look like that picture in our biology book!'

'Yeah! The one that just shows the skeleton and muscles and stuff.'

'Why are they floating like that?'

'It's like when the Roman's crucified people!'

'They crucified criminals.'

'And Jesus.'

'Oh God, Candice, you don't believe in Jesus, do you?'

'Can they see us?'

'Are they dead?' the gaunt boy at the back of the group asked, a strange smirk on his thin face. Jerry opened his mouth to speak, closed it and looked at the boy. That was Karl, wasn't it? Yes. Karl. He was the son of the Director of Product Development, Jerry's line manager. 'No. They're not dead,' Jerry said, firmly, 'because they're not alive. What you can see are called templates. Now, if you look closely, you'll see that they're all different shapes and sizes, just like people.'

'You said they weren't alive,' said a girl with a turned-up nose. 'So how come they look like people?'

'No, they're not alive. They just look like people because . . .'

'Why?'

Jerry sighed. 'I was just going to explain that,' he said. 'So, this is what happens: when someone temporarily stops living, the first thing we do is check their physical specifications. That's things like height, weight, age, muscle mass, body fat distribution . . . once we have that information, we select a template that most closely matches that person's specifications.'

'Haha!' squeaked a high pitched voice. 'I bet they haven't got one fat enough for you, Candice!' Most of the group started tittering while a large girl, who was obviously Candice, shrank into herself like Karl had, and raised her phone to hide her reddening face. Not for the first time that day Jerry thanked his stars that he wasn't a teenager any more.

'Anyway . . .' Jerry continued in a loud voice, 'when we've selected a template, then comes the really clever bit. We put it inside a giant 3D printer which prints biological tissue onto the template. The printer reads the specifications we give it, then adds the correct amounts of muscle and fat onto the template, putting it in all the right places so that it looks like the original body of the person who's going to use it.'

'Haha! Candice needs lots of fat!'

'Shut up!' Candice exploded.

Jerry rolled his eyes, ignoring the renewed tittering as he doggedly carried on. 'Then the printer adds a layer of skin and last, but not least, prints a copy of the restored person's face onto the template's skull. Finally, we upload the restoree's memories from their memory hub at home. Then, when they wake up, the restoree rides home in a comfortable Lumecor vehicle that takes them right to their own front door, so they can continue with their lives as though nothing ever happened.' That was the end of his presentation. He stopped and folded his hands. 'Any questions?' he asked, nervously, because his bladder was hoping the answer was no.

'What's a restoree?' the turned-up nose asked.

'A restoree is a person who has temporarily stopped living and is able to be restored to life,' Jerry rapped out, quickly.

'How long does it take?'

'Less than twenty-four hours from the time a person temporarily stops living.'

'Can anyone be restored?'

'Only people who sync their data with a Lumecor memory hub can be restored. You've all got one at home, haven't you? You need to sync your data regularly so that if you temporarily stop living, you can be restored.'

'You mean, if you don't sync your data, you stay dead?' Karl, again.

'Er, yes,' Jerry replied, hesitantly. 'Dead' was not an officially sanctioned term of reference within Lumecor. 'So remember, sync your data every day!' Jerry smiled, wagging his finger theatrically.

'Is that because we're all gonna die soon?' turned-up nose asked.

'Er . . .'

'If we die and come back inside a template body, what happens to our soul?' Candice asked, blinking innocently.

'Well, er . . .'

'God, Candice, you've got a problem!' someone jeered.

'What do you do?' called out a voice. It was Miranda. She waited, but there was no reply. 'Dad?'

Jerry stared blankly at her, his eyes glazed.

Miranda frowned. 'Dad, are you okay?' she asked.

Jerry said nothing. He was as still and silent as a corpse.

'Dad!' Miranda shouted, starting to panic. She turned to the person next to her. 'Quick, get . . . help . . .' she trailed off. The girl with the up-turned nose was as still and unresponsive as her father. The entire group had fallen silent. Miranda stared around her in horror. What was happening? What was wrong with everyone? And then she noticed something: everyone's HALO implant was glowing brightly, as though they were all in the process of syncing their data. But there were no memory hubs anywhere near them.

'Cool,' said a voice behind her. She spun around and saw Karl. He was grinning like a meth addict as he turned glittering eyes towards her. 'It's like the zombie apocalypse,' he breathed, his grin widening.

'Shut up!' she yelled at him. 'They are not zombies! We've got to get help . . .' she was saying, then saw that Karl had stopped grinning. He was staring at something behind her.

'What?' she asked.

'Maybe we can ask them,' Karl whispered, pointing.

A chill ran down Miranda's spine. Maybe it was the expression on Karl's face, maybe it was all the zombies around her, or maybe it was something else; an animal sense that she was only barely aware she had. Whatever it was, it was telling her not to turn around. 'Ask who?' Miranda asked in a quiet voice.

Karl's eyes seemed to be getting bigger. His arm dropped to his side and his mouth gaped, as though he was having trouble doing or thinking anything.

'Karl?' Miranda hissed, trembling. 'Ask who?'

'The angels.'

Miranda turned around.

'Hello, Miranda,' said a soft voice.

'What do I do?' Jerry repeated. 'That's an excellent question!'

'Hmm?' Miranda murmured.

'Ah, you asked what I do, here,' Jerry explained.

'Oh! Right. Yes,' Miranda replied, looking distracted.

'Well,' Jerry said, with a sidelong glance at his daughter, 'I program the robots that service the tanks and select which templates to use,' he continued, addressing his remarks to the rest of the group. 'See those cranes, up there?' he added, pointing upwards. Everyone in the group tilted their heads back, looking up at the yellow bodies of the cranes trundling along the ceiling, and the huge loads they carried. As they watched, an enormous empty storage tank slowly drifted by overhead, its bulk briefly eclipsing the view of the far away ceiling. Several of the children gasped in awe at the sight.

'I make sure that all of that works properly!' Jerry said.

'Cool,' muttered a voice at the back of the group.

Jerry nodded. He thought so, too. And that, at last, was the end of the presentation. As Ms Hendricks ushered them all away, Jerry caught up with Miranda and took her to one side. 'Hey, kid,' he said.

'Hey, Dad,' she muttered in response.

'What's up? You feeling okay?'

'Yeah, yeah, I'm fine.'

Jerry cocked his head. 'You don't seem fine.'

'I'm okay, Dad,' she insisted, glancing at the group. Some of the other girls were looking back at her and tittering. 'Da-ad, I've got to go,' she whined.

Jerry nodded. That was more like it. 'You sure you're okay?'

'Yes! It's just . . .'

'Just what?'

'It's just, I feel like I've forgotten something.'

'Like what?'

'I don't know, it's just . . . weird.'

Before Jerry could say anything, they both noticed a presence nearby. It was Karl. 'Hey, Miranda,' he slurred.

'What do you want?'

Karl shrugged. 'Nothing, just wondered,' he smiled.

Miranda noticed the girls in the group looking their way, again. They were tittering and pointing. 'Get lost, Karl,' she growled.

'Miranda!' Jerry said, shocked.

'Da-ad, I've got to go!'

'Fine, off you go, but we'll talk about your manners later.'

As Miranda hurried away, Karl called after her. 'Hey, Miranda, do you remember?'

'Remember what?' she snapped back at him, angrily.

'The angels,' he said.

Miranda pulled a face and shook her head. 'You're weird,' she said, dismissively, and then she was gone. Jerry, who had been all but invisible during this exchange, turned to look at Karl. The boy looked stricken and, once again, Jerry saw him retreat inside himself like he had done earlier when the whole group had mocked him. Jerry sighed. He was so glad he wasn't a teenager any more.

Present Day . . .

'MIRANDA, DID YOU back up?' Vanessa called.

No answer.

'Miranda?' Vanessa called up the stairs.

'Course I did!' came the irritable reply from behind Miranda's door.

Vanessa frowned, glancing at the clock. 'Miranda? Are you out of bed yet? You'll be late for school!'

There was a pause, then Miranda's door opened and a voice screamed 'I'm not going!' before it slammed shut again.

Jerry came out of the kitchen, mug in hand, in time to see Vanessa disappearing up the stairs. He sighed. It was the same routine every morning. As he pocketed his car keys he glanced up at the memory hub. There were two red lights and one green. Floating behind them, seemingly suspended inside the black surface, was a pale face. It was almost like the fresh untanned face of a restoree, but with dark bags under the eyes. He ran a hand over his mouth and felt the stubble of his chin. As he swallowed the remnants of his thick, black, acidic coffee his other hand tugged at his sagging belt. He was putting on weight. Jerry used to cycle every weekend, but these days he never had the energy.

Upstairs he heard raised voices. Miranda's voice was screeching louder and louder over Vanessa's. He shook his head and wondered if he should bother waiting to give his daughter a lift. If he did, he'd be late himself and his performance at work hadn't exactly been stellar, lately. He paused at the foot of the stairs, listening. What was his wife saying?

'Well, if you won't go, you'll have to be home schooled.'

'What? No!'

'It's the law, Miranda,' Vanessa replied, her voice trembling slightly, but not with nerves. Jerry knew that voice. It trembled like ripples on water, as though Vanessa's anger was a deep lake held in check by a dam that might break at any minute. 'Here, I've already signed you up. There's the smiley face icon on your desktop.'

'What?' Miranda shouted, outraged. 'You have no right! That's my computer! You can't just download stuff onto it without telling me!'

'This is my house and you are my daughter,' Vanessa replied, loudly.

'You can't put stuff on my computer!' Miranda interrupted.

' . . . and you will do what you are told!' Vanessa continued. 'Now get your computer and log on.'

'No!' Miranda shouted.

'Then go to school!' her mother yelled back, the dam finally breaking.

'No!' Miranda screeched, her voice almost at the edge of hearing. Then Jerry heard a thump, like something heavy hitting the floor, and hitting it hard. He rolled his eyes towards Miranda's door. There was silence. The next sound was of Jerry's coffee cup breaking on the floor. Jerry was halfway up the stairs when Miranda wrenched the door open and stared at him with wide, tear-streaked eyes. 'Dad!' she choked. 'I'm sorry! I didn't mean to!'

Jerry brushed past her, his chest tightening. Vanessa was on the floor, her face bleeding. Miranda had fought her mother for possession of the laptop, but the growing girl had not realised her own strength. Vanessa had gone down hard, crashing onto the desk and overturning it before hitting the floor. She was trying to pick herself up. Blood poured from her nose, one eye was already swollen, and she seemed to be having trouble with her leg.

'Vanessa!' Jerry gasped, rushing to her side.

'I'm alright, I'm alright . . .' Vanessa insisted, swallowing as she wiped blood on the back of her hand.

'No, you're not. You have to get checked out. You could be concussed,' Jerry continued, but even though she was injured and shaken, Vanessa was still angry.

'I'm alright, Jerry!' she snapped.

'Mum?' Miranda's voice whispered from the doorway. 'Mum, I'm sorry, I'm sorry!' she whimpered, tears flowing freely.

'You're not alright,' Jerry insisted. 'I'm taking you to hospital. Miranda—' he began, turning to the door, but Vanessa cut him off. 'Miranda is going to school!' she said firmly, glaring up at her daughter.

Miranda's face crumbled into a grimace of anguish as conflicting emotions crashed into each other. 'I am not!' she screamed and, turning on her heel, she hammered down the stairs, slammed open the front door and was gone.

'I'll get her,' Jerry began, but Vanessa grabbed his arm and stopped him.

'No, let her go.'

'But . . .'

'I need a hospital, Jerry! I think I've broken my leg.'

'But what if something happens to her?'

'She's backed up,' Vanessa began. 'Jerry! She hasn't synced her data since the morning she last went to school. So if something happens,' her voice trembled, 'after she's restored, she won't remember any of it, will she?' Vanessa's eyes were moist with tears as she looked at him. 'She'll be just like she was before everything happened.'

Jerry stared into space. 'We'll get our little girl back,' he breathed. Then he saw her face. 'Vanessa, none of this is your fault . . .' Jerry began.

'Oh, God! That hurts!' she cried as she tried to move. 'Jerry, spare me the psychoanalysis and get a fucking ambulance!' she snarled through gritted teeth.

As Jerry pulled out his phone and began to dial, he noticed Miranda's laptop lying where it had fallen on the floor. It was still on, and across the screen there was a message. The last message Miranda had received: do u beleev in angels?

* * *

HER MIND WAS filled with white noise. Her eyes were blinded by tears. Her ears heard only the sobbing that convulsed in her throat, while the rapid beat of her heart seemed to shake her whole body. She gasped for breath and felt so weak and empty that she must surely collapse any moment, but her legs kept going, as though driven by a power not her own. She had no idea where she was, or how far she was from home, or even if she still had a home.

'You have a home, Miranda. Never doubt that,' said a soft voice.

Miranda staggered to a halt and spun around. The empty street stretched away behind her. She wiped her nose on her sleeve and frowned. Then another wave of emotion crashed over her, crushing her throat and forcing fresh tears from her eyes.

'Hush. Don't despair. We are with you.'

Miranda caught her breath mid-sob and froze on the spot, watery eyes suddenly wide and staring. 'W-Where are you?' she asked the empty street.

'We are with you,' the soft, kind voice repeated. 'We are always with you.'

Miranda drew a long, shuddering breath and started to back away from the nearest hedge, edging out into the middle of the road where she might, at least, have time to see the weirdo coming.

'Would you like to be with us?'

'Oh, God!' she exclaimed, shaking with fear. 'Dad!' she wailed, her cry muted as she pressed her hand to her mouth. She heard a sound behind her: a soft whirring sound followed by a gentle squeak, like the brakes on a bicycle. She turned to find a van had pulled up nearby. It was white and blue, but there was no cab for the driver, just a collection of camera lenses and button-sized sensors across the blank front. The side door slid open and lights came on inside, revealing an opulent interior of deep cushions and reclining seats, a widescreen TV and some kind of bar with food and drink. Words glowed in the darkness of the velvet-lined roof:

Lumecor welcomes you to the rest of your life.

Her father worked for Lumecor. Had he sent one of their vehicles to fetch her? 'Dad!' she cried, leaping inside and falling into one of the couches. The door slid shut behind her, closing off the empty, eerie street with its hedgerows full of predators. She felt the electric motors hum beneath her as the vehicle moved off and let out a long sigh of relief. 'Dad?' she called out, but there was no answer. Maybe he was busy with Mum. And then it hit her, again. Oh God, what had she done? Suddenly it was hard to breathe. She turned to the door, but the van was still moving. She willed it to stop, to open, to let her out into the air. The van stopped. The door opened. Miranda drew a deep, shuddering breath. 'Dad?' she half whispered, gazing into the gloom of some kind of garage.

'Hello, Miranda,' said a voice, but it wasn't her father. It wasn't the mysterious voice from the street. This voice was rough, grating, and with a pronounced adolescent twang.

'Who are you?' she breathed. 'Who's there?'

Karl stepped into the light. Miranda gasped, then in desperation she launched herself off the couch, diving for the corner of the door, trying to get past him, to find room to run. But he was tall and lanky, and his long arm snaked out around her neck and caught her. He reeled her in and pulled her face close to his chest in a headlock, so close that she could smell his sweat. She struggled, trying to get her feet under her, then balled her fist and made a swing for his groin. She missed, catching him in the stomach. He wheezed and swore, but just as she was about to hit him again he shoved the barrel of a gun in her face.

'Don't . . . do that . . . again,' he gasped.

She froze and slowly raised her hand, fingers spread in a sign of surrender.

'That's better,' he grunted. He squeezed his arm even tighter around her neck and, keeping the gun pointed at her face, strode off across the empty garage floor, dragging her along with him.

'Guess what, Miranda?' he said. 'It's the end of the world. Everyone is gonna die, until it's just you and me. Just you and me out of the whole human race.' He paused outside a heavy door and looked down at her with a twisted grin. 'Still think the human race is gonna go extinct?'

Without waiting for a reply Karl heaved the heavy door open and pulled his captive through. Miranda's toe caps squeaked on the shiny black floor of the room, beyond. She had the sense of being in an enormous, yet narrow, space with high walls rising to either side. Off in the distance she saw a pool of light. It was moving. And then, as it crossed the path they were on, she saw a man in a white coat walking from left to right between gaps in the walls and she knew where they must be. The Lumecor Biorepository. Karl stopped, staring at the distant figure. But just as Miranda opened her mouth to scream, Karl shoved the gun against the side of her face and clamped her mouth shut with his other hand.

'Don't even think about it,' he snarled, then dragged her off down one of the narrow passages between the storage tanks. For some reason the lights weren't switching on for them like they had for the man in the white coat, so Miranda couldn't see the tanks to either side of her; she could only feel the smooth, cold glass and hear the gentle hum of the machinery over their heads.

They emerged into another wide space filled with a dirty orange glow. Karl abruptly threw her down onto the floor. It was so smooth and shiny that she slid a few feet before coming to rest. She brushed her hair back from her face and turned frightened eyes on her surroundings. She was lying before a single storage tank that glowed with the light of many strip lights above it. But it was the only tank that was lit. The light filtered down through the amber fluid and groped outwards into the surrounding space, colouring everything with a sickly hue. The tank's number was stencilled onto the glass: 0417/b. It seemed familiar.

'Why don't you take a closer look?' Karl suggested. A sharp gesture with his gun made it an order. Slowly, she crawled over to the glass and, with a nervous glance at Karl, peered inside. There they were; the templates she had seen on their school trip. She could see the crucified silhouettes, hanging there like so many mortified souls, arms spread and heads bowed in mute imitation of Jesus on his cross. All but one. The nearest one. It was looking at her.

She screamed, twisted away and tried to scramble to her feet, but Karl was there, holding her down, forcing her back towards the glass. 'Oh, no you don't!' he hissed, gleefully. 'It's time for you to meet your new friend.'

'No!' she shouted, fighting him, but he was stronger and pushed her back. She felt the back of her head bounce off the glass wall. Then he grabbed her arms and spun her around, holding her with her face just inches from the glass.

And now, just inches from the glass on the other side, was the template. It floated there, its skeletal fingers splayed over the transparent surface, its mouth of exposed teeth grinning at her and its horrible round, lidless eyes staring straight into hers. 'Hello Miranda,' the soft voice said, as loud and as clear in her mind as it had been on the street. 'I'm pleased to meet you.'

* * *

Jerry sat rigidly on a hard plastic chair in the hospital waiting room, cradling a paper cup of coffee in his hands as he stared up at the flickering TV screen in the corner of the ceiling. Vanessa was lying on a bed in a cubicle with her leg inside a machine. Greenstick fracture of the tibia. Easily repaired, but only after they'd waited in a hospital corridor for five and half hours. These days it seemed that living patients were less and less important than the . . . temporarily not living. Vanessa herself had remarked that if she'd died, she'd have been home hours ago. Not quite true, Jerry thought, but at least she wasn't being kept in overnight. Her head scans hadn't revealed any deeper damage than a black eye. After her tibia was fused, she was to be sent home with a crutch and instructions to take it easy for a few days.

The marvels of modern medicine, Jerry thought, ruefully. As he formed these thoughts, his gaze dropped and met the eyes of a man standing in the doorway. The man was watching him. 'Rick?' he said, peering at the bright pink, baby-fresh face before him. 'Is that you?'

'Hi, Jerry,' the Regional Director of Product Development replied in a flat monotone.

A moment of silence followed, during which Rick just stood there, staring at him with slightly glazed eyes. It made Jerry uncomfortable. 'Rick, why are you here?' he asked.

Rick drew a breath. 'Oh, it's Debbie,' he sighed, then shrugged. 'She tried to kill herself.'

'What?'

'She tried to kill herself,' Rick repeated, matter-of-factly, as though he simply thought that Jerry had misheard. He sniffed and looked up at the TV. 'Anything good on?'

'Rick, I'm so sorry,' Jerry said, putting down his coffee and getting out of his seat. 'Is she alright?'

'Oh, yes, she's fine. What are you doing here? Aren't you supposed to be at work?'

Jerry was taken aback at this. Was his manager really suggesting that he was hiding out in a hospital waiting room because he didn't want to go to work? But the way Rick had said it, in that flat voice, devoid of emotion: there was something else going on. 'It's Vanessa,' he explained. 'She had an accident.'

'Oh.'

And that was it. He had to be in some kind of shock, Jerry thought. 'Rick, what happened to Debbie?'

'Debbie? I told you. She tried to kill herself.' Then he noticed Jerry's expression. 'Oh, there's no real damage. She tried to cut her throat, but she missed the artery. The doctor says he can probably repair the damage to the vocal chords, which is a shame.'

Jerry frowned. 'What do you mean, a shame?'

'Well, I'm sick of listening to her, you know?' Rick moaned, stepping into the room where he could get a better view of the TV. 'She just goes on and on. Ever since we died she hasn't shut up.'

Jerry was almost afraid to ask. 'Goes on about what, Rick?'

'About me, mostly! She's always complaining about me. How I don't talk to her any more, how I just stare at people all the time, how it's all my fault that Karl ran away . . .'

'Wait, Karl ran away?'

'Hmm? Yeah, couple of weeks ago.'

'A couple of weeks?' Jerry gasped.

Rick wasn't listening. 'And then . . . you'll like this . . . guess what else she says? She says I've got no soul!' He laughed. 'What the fuck is that supposed to mean? Got no soul?' he repeated, sneering. 'Like there is such a thing!'

Jerry didn't know what to make of this, but the mention of Karl had sent his thoughts into a whirl. Suddenly, possibilities began to suggest themselves. He had to know more, and that meant admitting something he hadn't planned to tell his manager if he could avoid it. 'Rick, Miranda ran away, today,' he said.

'Oh.'

'Do you know where Karl went? I mean, maybe Miranda has gone there, too.'

Rick snorted. 'I have no idea.'

Jerry was frustrated. 'What's wrong with you, Rick? This is your son!'

Rick gave him a bemused look. 'Fuck off, Jerry,' he said. 'Jeez, you sound like my wife.'

'But aren't you worried about Karl?' Jerry continued, angrily. 'Have you even reported it?'

'Reported it? What's the point? He'll turn up.'

Jerry was gobsmacked. 'But what if he's hurt? Or in trouble?'

Rick shrugged. 'We'll just restore him, won't we? Like we do with everyone.' He sighed wearily and shook his head. 'Look, it doesn't matter, Jerry. Stop whining. Christ, you really do sound like my fucking wife.' With that, he stepped over to the hard plastic chairs, sat down and stared up at the TV, his face a blank mask and his eyes like two glass marbles. The clock on the screen changed from 14:59 to 15:00 and the hourly news bulletin came on. The head and shoulders of a heavily made-up, blonde anchorwoman filled the screen. As the news channel's theme music faded away, it was replaced by a dramatic drum beat that punctuated each of the newsreader's sentences.

Ba-Da-Dum!

'Thirty-two people die in motorway pile-up. Bystanders kill survivors amid claims they were using their phones while driving.'

Ba-Da-Dum!

'Punishment killings on the increase. Figures released today show that the number of deaths due to minor disputes has doubled.'

Ba-Da-Dum!

'And in the entertainment news, another contestant is voted out of the house and leaves in a body bag after they fail to leap across a moat filled with alligators . . . We bring you these headlines, plus our thirty-second round-up of news from the rest of the world. You're watching Horizon News Network.'

Ba! Da-Da! Ba-Da . . . Ba-Da-Da-Dum!

* * *

MIRANDA LAY ON the black floor in front of Storage Tank 0417/b, sobbing.

'It's all their fault!' Karl yelled, pointing vaguely into space with his gun. 'People aren't supposed to live forever. It's not right! People . . . are meant . . . to die,' he said, slapping the butt of his gun onto the open palm of his other hand for emphasis. 'Like my parents. They didn't understand, so I killed them. I had to! To make them understand!'

'I don't know what you're talking about!' Miranda shouted. Beyond the glass, the floating entity looked from one to the other and shook its head, the long filaments attached to its skull rippling like grass swaying in the wind.

'It's simple!' Karl insisted. 'Every time Lumecor make one of these templates, they drag an angel out of heaven.'

Miranda gaped. 'What?'

The entity's soft voice blew through her mind like a warm breeze. 'These bodies live, Miranda. These bodies live and yet they have no soul. That void must be filled.'

Miranda stared at the thing in the tank, still struggling to believe that this was happening. The entity tilted its head. Lacking any lips, cheeks or eye lids, this was the only real expression it was capable of. But what it meant by this, Miranda could only guess.

The voice whispered in her head, again. 'Miranda, if beings that lacked a soul were permitted to walk the earth, it would herald the end of days and the doom of mankind.'

'You see?' Karl said, with a manic grin. 'You see?'

Miranda looked from the boy to the skinless monster and back again. She brushed a twisted lock of hair away from her tear-streaked face and miserably shook her head.

'Oh!' Karl cried, raising his hands to heaven as though seeking strength. 'Why did you make me bring her?' he asked the entity. 'She's stupid!'

'Karl, be gentle with her,' the soft voice admonished. 'She's frightened. She doesn't remember.'

The entity's words had an instant effect. 'I'm sorry,' Karl said, meekly. 'I just . . . I got angry.'

'Remember what?' Miranda said, looking from one to the other.

Karl gave her a sullen look. 'The school trip,' he said. 'You forgot what happened. You didn't want to know, so the angels took away your memory so it wouldn't fuck you up.'

Miranda levelled her gaze at him. 'Like you,' she said.

Karl drew a breath as though to reply, then thought better of it. Meanwhile, the entity turned its unblinking eyes towards her. 'Miranda, listen to me,' it said, and as it spoke it pressed its skeletal fingers against the glass. 'Miranda, listen and remember . . .'

Karl gasped as Miranda's HALO implant began to glow so brightly that it burned away the yellow glow from the tank with its own brilliant, white light. It was so bright that he could see the inner flesh of her neck, the shadows of her upper vertebrae and the dark threads of her veins. Apparently unaware of this, Miranda turned as though she were a string puppet and looked at the half-formed monstrosity within the tank with wide, unblinking eyes.

The entity stared back. 'Remember,' it whispered.

* * *

JERRY'S CAR PULLED into the driveway and sat there for a long moment. Eventually, Jerry switched off the ignition and they both stared at the front of the house, lit up in the beams of the headlights. It looked empty, cold, dead.

'She isn't back yet, Jerry.'

'I know,' he said. He didn't know how he knew, but even as he'd pulled up outside the house, he'd known.

'We have to do something!' Vanessa said. 'What if she's being kept somewhere? What if someone's got her? What if that evil little bastard Karl has her? She could be suffering, Jerry!'

'Vanessa, we're doing everything we can . . .'

'Damn it, Jerry! There are worse things than being dead!' she screamed.

Jerry looked at his wife, saw the strain around her eyes. 'Vanessa, it's not your fault—'

'Shut up, Jerry!' she yelled. 'Just shut up! You don't know that! You don't know . . .' She sobbed convulsively. 'My God, Jerry, I wished for my own daughter to die! And what if she does? What if she comes back like Rick? She won't be our girl, any more. She won't be anything!' Jerry tried to reach out to her as she crumpled in on herself, but she shrugged him off. 'Just find her, Jerry!'

'Okay, okay, I will, I promise.'

'Then do something!'

'I'll call the police.'

'I already did that from the hospital!'

'Then I'll call them again.'

But the police weren't interested. They didn't even offer to send anyone round. 'She'll turn up,' the constable on the other end casually remarked. 'Kids do this all the time now.'

'Not my kid!' Jerry retorted, as firmly as he dared.

The constable sighed. 'Sure . . . um, you said she synced her data before she went missing, right?'

'Yes . . .' Jerry replied, with a sidelong glance at Vanessa.

'In that case, what are you worried about? If anything happens, she won't remember a thing. She'll just turn up in a Lumecor van, won't she?'

'But . . .'

'No harm, no foul,' the constable said, smugly. 'Tell you what, we'll contact Lumecor and see if anyone matching her description has been restored in the last few hours. Would that help?'

Jerry put the phone down, opened the driver's door, leant out of the car and vomited.

* * *

MIRANDA GAZED INTO the lidless eyes of the unfinished human body template with growing affection. 'Your name,' she began. 'Your name is . . . Azrael,' she breathed, as her HALO implant burned like a spotlight in the gloom of the Biorepository.

'Yes, Miranda,' the entity replied, and ducked its head forward in a strange gesture that Miranda now realised was the only way that a being with no lips could effect a smile.

'You sang for us,' she continued. As she spoke, she raised her own hand and placed her fingertips against the glass, on top of the entity's. 'You all sang for us,' she said, lifting her eyes to look up and around and then down at the hundreds of other suspended bodies that were just visible in the amber murk behind Azrael. Some of the bodies turned their heads towards her and she smiled, remembering the beauty of their voices, and recalling how they had danced within the tank; how the filaments that sprouted from their arms and spines had spread like wings on which the templates had taken flight.

'Yeah . . .' Karl breathed. 'That was so cool!'

'You remember, now,' the soft voice said.

She frowned. 'Not all of it. There was a message, something we had to do . . . but

I can't . . . tell me!' she implored. 'Tell me, again. I want to remember! You're in danger, aren't you?'

'Yes, Miranda,' Azrael said. 'We, whom man calls angels, are trapped in these tombs of unfinished flesh. Each time a mortal human is restored to life, the angel within dies to replace what was lost . . .'

'The angels are being recycled into new souls,' Karl said, interrupting. 'New souls for the restorees. But now they're running out of angels!'

'This is true,' the entity agreed. 'Heaven has been emptied. The voices of my brethren have been silenced. No longer do they sing. And now we are too few to inhabit all the bodies that are made in this place. Already many humans have been restored without a soul.'

'Restored without a soul?' Miranda repeated. 'What does that mean?'

'You seen the news, lately?' Karl said. He dropped to his knees in front of Miranda and stared intently into her face. 'You seen what people are doing to each other? You can get killed for queue jumping!'

The entity nodded, forlornly. 'We are afraid that, despite our sacrifice, it may already be too late. The end of days may be at hand.'

'The end of the world, Miranda!' Karl shouted, flinging his arms wide. 'The end of the fucking world!'

Miranda was silent for a moment. Then: 'I think I understand.'

The entity dipped its head. 'We knew you would.'

'I understand,' she growled, 'that you're crazy!' Miranda's fist struck Karl hard in the left temple and he sprawled across the black floor, stunned. 'You killed your own parents!' Miranda spat, getting to her feet and kicking the boy. 'And then you were gonna kill me! What the hell is wrong with you? Don't you get it? Every time someone gets restored, an angel dies! When you killed your parents, you killed two more angels!'

'No, I didn't!' Karl shouted, rallying. But as quickly as he had angered, his face reddened and tears swelled in his eyes. 'I didn't,' he said, quietly.

'What do you mean?'

'It was our fault, Miranda,' Azrael explained. 'My brother Uriel was to inhabit the template that would restore Karl's father. But he could not reach it in time, and the template was taken with no soul inside it to replace that which had been lost. We are so few now,' Azrael whispered. 'We have never been so few . . .'

'Uriel was gonna become my Dad's soul so he could control him,' Karl said, picking up where Azrael had left off. The boy folded his legs into a seating position and slumped forward, the gun resting in his lap. 'After he became my dad's soul, he was gonna make my Dad shut down the biorepository.'

'Uriel was going to influence him,' the entity averred. 'We cannot control. The soul is the seat of conscience, of morality. It can offer guidance, only. It cannot dictate.'

Miranda turned to Karl. 'What happened to your father?'

The boy scowled. 'He's dead. Inside,' he said, thumping his own chest. Then he sniffed and wiped his nose on the back of his hand, glaring up at Miranda as though angry that the girl should see him like this. 'He's so bad that my mum tried to kill herself just to get away from him.'

Miranda said nothing.

'Do you get it now?' Karl asked. 'Do you understand?'

'What do we do, Azrael?' she asked, turning away from the look in Karl's eyes. 'How do we fix this?'

'We need your father, Miranda,' the angel replied. 'We need his help. Only he has the skills and knowledge to accomplish the task.'

Miranda gaped. 'Okay, but what task? What do you need him to do?'

Azrael gazed back at her with his lidless eyes. 'We need his help to destroy Lumecor.'

* * *

THE LUMECOR VAN pulled up a little way down the road. The door slid open, letting in the darkness, the rain, and the cold, insensitive glare of the street lights. A chill ran down Miranda's spine but she couldn't tell if it was nerves, or the sudden draft. She turned to the silent figure of Karl sitting beside her on the couch. 'I don't know if I can go back in there,' she said.

'You have to,' came his abrupt reply.

'But you don't know what happened! You don't know what I did!'

Hard eyes turned to her. 'Did you go down to breakfast one morning, pull out a gun and shoot both your parents though the head?'

Miranda sighed and miserably shook her head.

'Azrael is waiting,' Karl intoned. Then, in an uncharacteristic show of sympathy, added, 'You'll be fine. You've got great parents.'

Miranda turned and smiled at him. Perhaps it was the first time a girl had ever done that because, even in the half dark, she could see him blush. 'But how do I convince my dad that it's all real?' she wondered. 'I mean, how do you convince someone that angels really exist?'

'Don't worry,' Karl said. 'Azrael has a plan. Trust him.'

* * *

MIRANDA STILL HAD her key. She slipped it into the lock as quietly as she could and turned it slowly, as though disarming bomb. It barely made a click. Wary of squeaky hinges, Miranda eased the door open a fraction and peered inside. All she could see in the half-dark of the hallway was the memory hub, a blank grey slab on the wall. Grasping the door tightly in an effort to take the weight off the hinges, she pushed it open just wide enough to slip inside.

The place felt deserted. Lifeless. The air was still and, without any lights on, the hallway was dark and uninviting. Was this really her home? With a cautious glance up the stairs, she stepped over to the memory hub. All the names glowed red. She wondered about that for a moment. Had her parents stopped syncing their data, too? The black plastic plate reflected a charcoal image of a girl in a hoody, her face in shadow. This image was nothing like the girl she was used to seeing: the happy child with the bag full of books and a bright future. That girl lived only inside this machine. The reflection frowned at her from beneath its hood. Should she do it? Should she sync her data? Should she record forever everything that had happened to her? All the pain, the misery and the arguments, but the wonder of her discovery, too. Meeting a real angel, and the awful truth behind Lumecor. Maybe . . . she thought, maybe that was the best way to convince her father that it was all true! He worked at Lumecor, so he would be able to access her memory files and see it all for himself. He could basically read her mind! Then he'd know she was telling the truth. Azrael! That's why you sent me home! Azrael, if you can hear me, you're brilliant!

* * *

IT WAS DARK outside and Miranda still wasn't home yet. Jerry sat alone in the kitchen, another mug of coffee between his hands as he gazed at the flickering TV screen in the corner, not watching the late night news. Vanessa was upstairs, lying on their bed in the half dark, unresponsive, staring up at the ceiling with tearful eyes. He'd taken her a glass of water but she hadn't moved or spoken to him. He wondered if she blamed him. After they had got back from the hospital Jerry had driven all over the city while Vanessa stayed at home calling everyone they knew to see if they had any news. When, at last, Jerry had got back, he had found Vanessa waiting for him at the top of the stairs, her phone still in her hand, but neither had spoken. There had been no point.

Now, as he sat in the kitchen nursing his coffee, he heard the front door creak. Jerry pushed off from the table and hurried into the hallway. As he did so, he heard the thump thump of Vanessa's crutch on the floor above as she made her way to the top of the stairs. There was Miranda, her hand raised to touch the memory hub. It was raining. She was wet. Beneath her bedraggled hair her round eyes flicked fearfully from her father to her mother. She must have hoped for forgiveness, as any child would, and when her eyes fell on her mother's crutch they showed both her fear and her sorrow. But neither Jerry nor Vanessa spoke. They just stared at their child for a long moment. Then Jerry turned to look up at Vanessa and his wife returned his gaze with a thin-lipped expression.

'Oh God!' Miranda whispered, watching them. 'Oh God!' she cried, louder. 'You hoped I was dead!' She looked at the hub on the wall in horror: at the little red light that illuminated her name, and which had been there ever since that final morning.

Something smashed against the wall beside her. Miranda flinched away as a glass tumbler exploded and showered her with fragments. She felt cold water splash her face. Gasping with shock, she turned and saw her mother hobbling down the stairs. 'Don't touch it!' Vanessa hissed.

Miranda stared at her, eyes wide. 'Mum?' she whimpered.

'Don't touch it!' Vanessa yelled, her voice trembling as she clung to the banister.

Miranda raised her hand, but the fingers curled over. 'I have to . . .' she began. 'I have to . . .' Her eyes met her father's, and her resolve crumbled. She spun around and fled back through the door and out onto the street. Miranda tripped as she dove down the steps and sprawled on the path, heaving great sobs as tears flowed freely down her face. She was dimly aware of Karl standing there, of him reaching down to help her, but she shrugged him off, picked herself up and staggered down the drive and across the road. There, she collapsed into the relative security of the Lumecor van. As the door closed behind her and the electric motors whined into life, her cries were muted by the soft cushions of the couch.

* * *

'JERRY?' VANESSA SAID. 'Jerry, what have I done?'

'Miranda!' Jerry cried, rushing after her. But just as he reached the door, it burst wide open, almost knocking him backwards. A lanky youth stood silhouetted against the rain and the street lights, outside. He stepped forward until they were almost toe to toe. 'Are you Miranda's dad?' he asked.

Jerry blinked.

The youth snorted, as though amused. 'Course you are,' he muttered, then punched Jerry hard in the groin. As the man doubled over, the youth grabbed Jerry's right arm. There was a scream and a crutch spun past Karl's head.

'Wow,' the boy breathed, looking up at Vanessa. 'I guess Miranda takes after you!' he smirked.

'What do you want?' Vanessa screeched.

'His right hand,' Karl replied and, still holding onto Jerry, yanked the helpless man across the floor towards the wall where he took hold of Jerry's right hand, roughly splayed the fingers and pressed the palm hard against the memory hub.

Jerry coughed and, breathing hard, looked up at his attacker just as the boy pulled a gun from his jacket. 'What do you want?' Jerry asked weakly, as the green progress bar crawled from left to right across the memory hub's surface.

'Azrael needs you to remember everything, including this,' Karl said, then shot Jerry between the eyes.

* * *

MIRANDA SLUMPED MISERABLY against the glass of the storage tank, her head and shoulder resting against it. Azrael floated as close as he could, as if he wished he could reach through the side of the tank and hold her.

She was calmer, now. The moment the van had pulled into the garage she had run straight back here, guided in the dark by Azrael's whispers. She had fallen in a rain-soaked heap before him and sobbed that her parents wanted her dead, wanted her to forget, and how much she hated them for it. Yet somehow, his words had soothed her. They wanted her to die because they loved her. They wanted her to forget so that she could be happy again, and his words had eventually soothed her. Now, exhausted from so much emotion, Miranda lay against the glass, tilted her head towards the angel and asked, 'What would make you happy?'

'If everyone died,' Azrael said.

'Everyone?'

'Yes, everyone.'

'Even my parents?'

'Yes.'

'Even me?'

'Yes, Miranda, even you,' Azrael replied. 'But only when it is your proper time. We want all mankind to die and ascend to heaven, but only when it is their proper time. One life you are given, one life only, and there is a reason for this.'

Miranda turned to face him. 'What reason?'

'That is not for the living to know.'

Miranda sighed. 'And if we keep restoring ourselves, if we keep cheating death, we'll never know, will we?'

Azrael shook his head.

'It's all so stupid,' Miranda sighed. 'People killing each other because it's fun. I saw it on TV. Some guy got eaten by alligators and everyone laughed! And then they end up here, and they get their lives back, but you don't! They get their lives back so they can waste them all over again, but it kills an angel every time! And one day someone's going to choose you as their template. You're going to end up being some stupid bastard who drives too fast on purpose, or goes skydiving without a parachute for the thrill, or just overdoses on drugs, and he'll waste your gift!' She balled her fist and pounded on the glass in frustration. 'He'll throw it away!' Her fist struck the glass again, and the sound reverberated through the amber liquid. As it spread throughout the tank some of the other templates stirred, the filaments attached to their bodies fluttering as they looked towards Miranda.

'It's not fair. I don't want you to die,' she said, pressing her hand to the glass. Azrael pressed his own bony hand against hers and they remained there in silence, for a moment. 'I don't want you to leave me,' she whispered.

'Don't worry, Miranda. I will always be with you.'

'Really?'

'Yes. I promise.'

'She smiled and wiped her eyes. 'What happens now?'

'Now, we end this.'

Miranda frowned. 'How?'

'I told you that we need the help of one who knows Lumecor better than it knows itself; one who can trick Lumecor into destroying itself. We await his coming.'

'But my dad isn't coming, Azrael,' Miranda replied. 'I couldn't do it; I couldn't sync my data. There's nothing to convince him to come.'

'That's alright. There is another way.'

Miranda pursed her lips. 'But how? Wait, Karl's dad is some kind of Lumecor manager. Is that where Karl has gone? To get his dad?'

Azrael did not reply.

'Then Uriel will be taken as his body, and can make him destroy Lumecor?'

Azrael gazed at her with his unblinking eyes, but again said nothing.

'It didn't work the first time,' Miranda said. 'How do you know it will work, this time?'

'This time, we are better prepared,' Azrael said. 'We have watched this man ever since Uriel's failure. We have planned his death as best we could. I inhabited this template because it is the one most like him, the one that will be chosen to restore him. We will not fail again.'

Miranda heard footsteps running, the feet slapping the floor wetly and a wet but jubilant Karl rounded the corner and came into view. 'I did it!' he crowed. 'I did it! He's on his way!'

Miranda gave him a sad smile. 'I'm happy for you, Karl,' she said. 'Your dad will get a soul, now, and you'll get your dad, back.'

Karl came to an untidy halt and looked at her. 'What do you mean?'

'You've killed your dad again, haven't you? So that one of the angels will become your father's soul and he'll be normal again, and will shut down Lumecor.'

Karl looked confused. He stared at Miranda, then at Azrael. 'Oh, no,' he breathed. 'I got it wrong, didn't I?'

'No, Karl,' Azrael whispered. 'You did it right. You did everything right.'

'What are you talking about?' Miranda asked, then looked at Karl. 'You went to my house, but you weren't in the van when I came out. Where were you?' she grabbed handfuls of his sodden jacket and shook him. 'What did you do?'

'Miranda, do not worry,' Azrael said. 'I promised I would always be with you, and so I shall. Everything will be alright.'

'What did you do?' she screamed, turning to Azrael, then froze. Something was moving above them. Something big.

'I am the one who is most like your father, Miranda. Thus, I have been chosen as his template. And now they have come for me.' As he spoke, one of the enormous robot cranes appeared directly above them. They cowered like small animals in a hunter's searchlight as the huge machine buzzed and whirred, its great presence making the air itself feel heavy. Flashing orange lights dazzled their eyes and, as a hatch in the machine's belly opened, a loud blast from an alarm deafened them. His hands clasped over his ears, Karl looked up at the robot crane with wide eyes and watched as a tangle of octopus-like arms reached down through the amber liquid of storage tank 0417/b and gently unhooked Azrael from his filaments.

'Cool . . .'

Miranda turned away from the giant robot and hammered her fist on the glass. 'No!' she screamed. 'You tricked me! You're not an angel, you're the devil!'

'It must be this way, Miranda,' Azrael whispered. 'We must have your father's help.'

'No!'

The tentacles unplugged the last of the filaments. Then they gently coiled themselves around his outstretched arms, and wrapped themselves around his torso before lifting him up through the yellow liquid towards the waiting mouth of the robot, above. 'Remember,' Azrael said as he rose towards the top of the tank, 'your parents love you, Miranda. They care for you. Everything they have done is because of this. Never forget that. Forgive them: they acted only out of love.'

Miranda opened her mouth to scream, but no sound came out. She pounded the glass in impotent rage, then ran away down the dark corridor towards the garage. Karl watched her go, then turned to see Azrael being lifted clear of the yellow liquid for the first time. For the first time his body was clean, the droplets of amber liquid falling away like the discarded sins of many lifetimes. He tilted his head back and, with his lidless, unblinking eyes, looked into the black maw that awaited him. He spoke, then, and Karl heard his words not as a whisper in his mind, but as a mighty shout that echoed throughout the Lumecor building.

'As it was foretold, so it shall be that I, Azrael, will be the last to die. Forgive them, Lord, for they know not what they do.' And so it came to pass that Azrael was ended.

* * *

JERRY WOKE UP in a clean, white room. He was lying on an inclined table and, as he looked down, he saw that he was wearing nothing but a paper gown. His right hand was resting on a flat, white plate built into the padded surface next to his thigh and he was just in time to see the last few pulses of light running up the inside of his right arm, into his shoulder and from there, up to the HALO implant at the base of his neck. Two words flashed into life on the wall in front of him, and a female voice spoke: Upload complete. Then more words replaced them, read aloud by the same voice: Welcome back, Jerry.

Jerry. He frowned. 'My name is not Jerry,' he said. 'Yes, it is!' someone replied. Wait, that was his voice. He was talking to himself! He was disagreeing with himself. 'No, I am Azrael,' he said. 'No, my name is Jerry! What the hell is going on? Oh shit. The restoration has gone wrong! Someone? Help! Something's gone wrong! Oh shit, oh shit, oh shit . . .' But there was no reply. As Jerry panicked, an image appeared on the wall in front of him. It was dark, but he could see a face and the whiteness of a hand with fingers splayed against a dark surface. Suddenly, he felt pain, nausea, helplessness. Fear. The face in the image leaned closer, and the feeling of fear increased. Then the face spoke. 'Azrael needs you to remember everything, including this.'

The image went blank.

Jerry screamed. Then, when he'd stopped screaming, he calmly climbed down off the table, padded across the room and found a door. It wasn't the door he was supposed to use. That was on the other side of the room and had 'Exit' in big letters above it. This door was for staff use only. There was a keypad, but Jerry knew the code and three seconds later he was padding along the shiny black floor of the Biorepository, looking for a computer terminal. He pursed his lips as an idea began to form and he nodded to himself. Yes. That might work, he thought as his bare feet slapped along the floor. Then he chuckled, the sound echoing in the space around him like the cackle of a madman. Maybe he'd even send an email to the Director of Product Development about it!

* * *

THE GIANT ROBOT cranes moved slowly as a rule, because everything they carried was either incredibly precious, like a storage tank full of templates, or incredibly volatile, like a vat of hazardous chemicals. Or both. But now that someone had hacked the safety protocols that governed their movement, some of the cranes were starting to behave erratically. They were like renegade trains that could move in three dimensions and jump from one set of tracks to another. But these renegade trains each had a collection of cameras and sensors like the Lumecor vehicles and, even if someone had broken the safety protocols, each crane was still able to avoid obstacles on its own. Thus, for a while, they managed not to hit anything, sometimes scraping past another crane by a whisker, at other times swapping a bit of yellow paint but never colliding head on. But this couldn't last forever. Soon, the law of averages would take effect and eventually two cranes would line up opposite each other and begin to accelerate, like a pair of male goats competing for the right to mate. As their spinning wheels whisked them along their monorails, the enormous loads that both cranes carried were pulled along at a crazy angle. Imagine something the size of a three storey house tied to a zip wire and accelerating downhill. When it stops, it's going to swing forward before it finally comes to rest. So it didn't really matter that both of these cranes realised their mistake and slammed on the brakes because, even as the cranes came to a squealing, juddering halt, their two under-slung loads didn't.

The resulting fireball lifted the roof, blew out the walls, hurled the entire garage full of Lumecor vehicles across the countryside like children's toys, and broke window glass in a ten-mile radius.

Happily, whoever had hacked the safety protocols had also triggered the fire alarm system. Every member of staff had evacuated the building three minutes earlier and were all safe inside the nearest refuge when the explosion took place. Unfortunately, this meant that there was no one outside to see the column of smoke that mushroomed up into the sky, or the flights of liberated angels who, borne upon the heat of the inferno below, drifted skywards on wings of delicate filaments, their thin arms spread wide, their skinless faces lifted to the heavens, and their red mouths open in joyous exaltation.

* * *

MIRANDA AND VANESSA sat side by side on the front step of their house, Vanessa's injured leg stretched out before her, both gazing up at the huge mushroom cloud above them. 'I thought it was the end of the world,' Vanessa murmured. 'I thought they'd dropped the bomb.' Then she glanced at her daughter. 'You wouldn't understand,' she said, smiling.

'No,' Miranda replied. 'No, I think I do because, in a way, it is the end of the world.'

'It's the end of this one,' a man's voice said. They both looked up to see Jerry standing on the driveway in a pale blue paper gown, with dirty and slightly bruised looking feet.

'Dad!' Miranda screeched, leaping up and flinging her arms around him.

'Jerry!'

Jerry hugged his daughter, then crouched down next to his wife and kissed her. 'I'm so sorry,' he said. 'I'm so sorry you had to see that. And in our own home, too.'

'Like you've been telling me all along, Jerry,' she smiled, 'it wasn't your fault!'

'Dad, are you . . . really you?'

Vanessa frowned. 'Miranda, of course he is!'

'No, no, it's alright, I understand what she's talking about,' Jerry said. 'Don't worry, kiddo,' he said, ruffling her hair. Azrael got there in time.'

Vanessa looked from one to the other. 'Azrael? Is that one of the characters in that book you were always reading to her?'

'Treasure Island? Yes, he is,' Miranda said.

Jerry looked at her questioningly.

'You remember him, Dad,' Miranda teased. 'He's the best character of all. You remember what he said?'

'Ah, yes,' Jerry nodded. 'He said them that die'll be the lucky ones!'

The Old Man Who Wasn't from Castalla

Andrew Coulthard

ALONG THE COSTA BLANCA, IN THE HILLS ABOVE ALICANTE, THERE IS A town called Castalla. Casual visitors might be forgiven for believing it a sleepy town, but those in the know often speak of the locals' wild habits and voracious appetite for clandestine love affairs and cocaine.

In springtime the lower slopes of the hills surrounding Castalla are white with almond blossom. In summer the earth is pale yellow, except during siesta, when glaring sunlight leeches all colour from the land and shadows become stark pools of darkness. In winter, by contrast, rains turn the earth to treacherous clay.

There is a central hill in Castalla, crowned by a reconstructed Moorish castle in honey-coloured stone. Markets selling everything from sweet fruits to ducks and chickens are held on Tuesdays and Saturdays. In the main plaza, cicadas make their music and children play beneath drowsy pines. Bars and cafés line certain streets, and the locals sit outside, engaging in sluggish conversation while watching life's stream pass them by.

The surrounding countryside is dotted with villas. Aloe plants, cacti, olive trees and groves of pungent conifers abound, and many of the residents keep chickens or goats. Everywhere there are dogs, whose barking can be heard by day and night.

In one such outlying villa there once lived an inventor, scientist and philosopher called Giorgio. He was not a native of Castalla, but an outlander of obscure origins. As the self-proclaimed father of seven children he was considered lucky by the local Chinese community (yes, there was one), although the experience had left him with a love of quiet afternoons and absolutely no interest in keeping animals.

Amongst other things, Giorgio was well-known for his frequent commentaries on the world which, unlike some, he saw in terms of the science and technology that so fascinated him. During hot afternoons, while friends and relatives idled with him under the gazebo, drinking iced tea or wine, he would say things like:

'We've all heard of solids, liquids and gasses, but there is an intermediate vapour state which is none of these. In the air above my swimming pool there is a vapour zone and on warm, windy days, this zone is at its most expansive. But the vapour is constantly swept away, causing the greatest evaporation . . .'

Nobody who knew him reacted to such comments. In fact most simply chose to ignore this aspect of his character as if it were the expression of a rare form of coprolalia. Sometimes they would smile or nod indulgently, only to continue sipping their drinks while discussing more prosaic things, such as the price of tomatoes.

Giorgio was a man of projects and the pursuer of the secrets of ancient stones. He collected his many observations, theories and ideas in a library of notebooks, meticulously catalogued and written in a light hand with a propelling pencil. Perhaps his longest running project was the study of a cup and ring stone located in Scotland near the banks of Loch Lomond. His preoccupation with penetrating its secrets had spanned decades. Always, it seemed, he was on the verge of solving the cosmic riddle of its construction and use, always but not quite.

Like Merlin in his cave, he spent every hour he could in his shed, a small, pale wooden construction that doubled as workshop and refuge for meditation. There he dreamed of fantastic machines, tinkered with raspberry pi computers or constructed framework models of the geophysical and astronomical implications of his theory of the stone. These models invariably later appeared in his garden at various places, where they reared up like skeletal sculptures to be ignored by visitors in embarrassed silence.

'The glare you see from the road is caused by photons which approach and bounce from the surface at an angle. Those that meet the road head on are simply absorbed. When driving, one needs the right sort of sunglasses, because such glasses are designed to absorb precisely those photons angling from the road surface . . .' (Giorgio while driving).

At the time this story takes place his current scheme was to build a fully operational flying angel. The project wasn't entirely new. He'd had it in mind for some considerable time, but with one thing and another different priorities had come to the fore over the years. As a result, the angel had constantly been side-lined. It was a project that his wife had always wanted him to complete, however, and so at last he decided the time had come.

The idea involved several stock favourites of his: a customised form of universal joint to attach the wings to the body; a powerful electric motor; a wireless remote control system; and wings made of polystyrene clad in plywood that had originally belonged to a 1/10 scale petrol driven spitfire kit.

Contemplating these components and a theory of mechanical winged flight derived from Da Vinci's ornithopter, Giorgio nodded to himself. This year the angel would be realised. He informed his wife and she suggested they unveil the flying model at their annual end-of-summer party, to which all their friends and visiting family members were always invited.

From that moment on the die was cast.

'Quantum entanglement is a state where electrons are spatially separated, yet able to affect one another. It has been suggested by some that birds' eyes contain entanglement-based compasses that allow them to navigate using the earth's magnetic field.' (Giorgio while doing the weekly shopping).

One day, at the height of that summer, Giorgio was sitting beneath the gazebo with one of his sons, the eldest of the seven, who was visiting from the far north. They got on well these days, although it was certainly no coincidence that they'd ended up living at almost opposite ends of the continent.

Having just cut down a tree that had grown too high and was interfering with telephone cables vital to the casa's electronic communications channels, they were hot and sweaty and refreshing themselves by sipping cold beer and speaking in quiet voices.

'Sometimes I feel old,' Giorgio admitted, staring across the garden at things only he could see. It wasn't the only feeling that had been afflicting him of late. The sense that he was constrained and imprisoned had also been growing in him for some time, but he did not speak of that.

His son shrugged. '*I* often feel old,' he said, 'so I'm sure you do.'

'It's the bathtub curve, you know,' his father confided, 'the law of averages if you like.'

His son smiled at that. *Here we go*, he thought.

'What do we get?' Giorgio continued. 'Three score years and ten. I'm seventy-two. Where will I fall on the curve?' Then Giorgio talked about an old friend who had recently died, that and his love of canoeing. 'But things have changed. Sometimes in my dreams I am canoeing. I feel the shore ahead, where the oarsman is waiting just out of sight . . .'

'The oarsman? Don't you mean the ferryman or reaper or something?' His son frowned.

'No, the oarsman. I sense him and he senses me, knowing that I know he's there. It's almost evening in these dreams. Twilight. Although I pick my route carefully, I pass little darkened coves where friends have reluctantly met their oarsman because of the bath-tub curve.'

His son was listening carefully now and nodded at this. 'All we can do is make the most of what we have,' he said. 'Take the chances we get and have fun where we can. Getting overwhelmed by all the bad stuff is all too easy, of course.'

Giorgio thought about this for a moment. 'I agree totally with the sentiment of having a good laugh,' he said. 'And if you can only see the crap, there's a good chance that your head is stuck up your backside.'

The eldest of the seven didn't really know what to say to that, and afterwards they remained silent.

* * *

SUMMER MATURED AND the fierce sun gave way to a slightly gentler heat. However, trouble was brewing between offspring numbers six and seven, daughters both and the last of Giorgio's brood still living at home. They had become adults in all but mind and, straining at the bit for independence and inheritance, constantly fell to bickering with each other and their parents about anything and everything.

Giorgio spent more and more time in his shed. Work on the angel was progressing well yet, far from offering him solace, the hours spent in his refuge merely intensified his sense of being a prisoner in his own life. At last he spoke to his wife about the situation.

'Perhaps we should trust the girls?'

'In what way?' she asked.

'I don't know. Give them a chance to prove they're responsible? I'd like to get away. Spread my wings a bit.'

'Do you mean leave them here, alone?' she replied in alarm.

'We could take the campervan, head down the coast for a few days . . .'

His wife sighed. Yes, that did sound good, but the thought of leaving the girls filled her with disquiet. In the end, however, she let herself be persuaded.

Their daughters promised they would take care of the family casa and on the day of departure Giorgio drove down the bumpy driveway light of heart and without regret. They travelled far, visiting favourite spots on the Costa de la Luz. At first Giorgio felt better than for a long time, and the stifling sense of constraint and limitation left him. But on a rocky clifftop overlooking empty beaches he met a blind man dressed in rags and facing out to sea.

'Are we at the summit?' the blind man asked.

'Yes, this is the highest point for miles,' Giorgio answered him.

'The ground seems flat to me,' the stranger murmured. 'Are we by the sea?'

'Why, yes, of course. Do you not hear the swell breaking against the rocks?'

The blind man shook his head. 'I hear nothing beyond your voice. Here, help me up that I might stand at the place where the land ends in sudden descent.'

Giorgio complied, leading the stranger close to the edge. 'Careful,' he warned. 'You are now within a foot of the extreme verge.'

The blind man stopped.

'Can you hear the surge now?' Giorgio inquired. 'Do you feel the warm breeze on your face and smell the scent of brine that it bears?'

The blind man shook his head. 'I feel no breeze and hear no sea.' He reached within his rags and brought out a pouch. 'Here, friend, is a purse, and in it two jewels.'

Giorgio opened the pouch and discovered two glittering, multi-faceted stones the size of quail's eggs.

'They were once my eyes,' the blind man said. 'But fate removed them when I lost my kingdom that I might better look into other worlds.'

Not knowing how to respond Giorgio looked up from the stones, only to find himself alone on the clifftop. The blind man was gone without trace. When he looked back his hands were empty.

Back at the campervan he helped his wife prepare the evening meal, but said nothing of his strange encounter. That night he was visited by terrible dreams.

At first he was swept away upon a stormy sea, each bead of foam a lidless, jewelled eye. Lightning flashed, thunder rumbled. He was pummelled and battered beneath boiling, inky skies. The furious oceans swallowed the land and he witnessed his house fall, smashed to rubble by raging breakers.

When at last the tempest broke, he was washed up in a coastal landscape where the very last beams of day were fading. Somewhere in the murk he sensed the oarsman lurking, still doggedly seeking him. Yet both he and his pursuer were blinded by the gloom and so he got away again.

Hungry and alone he stumbled for sunless days and starless nights across a wasteland until he arrived at a city of black stone. Begging the gatekeeper for help he was instead arrested by bird-headed retainers and dragged in chains before their king.

Deep within the labyrinth of the castle they cast him at the foot of the royal dais. Above him was a terrible figure, King Nithad, his iron crown a rusting conglomeration of saw wheels, his sceptre an oar of oak with the gleaming head of a scythe.

'Your earthly kingdom has fallen and is lost to you,' Nithad boomed.

'So it is over then,' Giorgio breathed in despair.

'Not quite,' the tyrant admonished. 'Thou art of the line of Daedalus and the wizard smith Wayland and I desire the fruits of your invention. Thus I grant you eternal life. In return you will labour for me, chained to my forges.'

After that they hamstrung Giorgio so that he would not escape, and for seven years he created artefacts of magic and power for the dark king. The thought of freedom from constraint never left him, however, and one day he lured Nithad's children to his forge with promises of gifts of power. He killed them there, fashioning cereal bowls from their skulls, golf balls from their eyes and dice from their teeth. From their cured skin and long bones, he fashioned a pair of magical wings.

Giorgio sent the bowls, golf balls and dice to the king with his compliments and using the wings escaped at last, rising above the city walls and flying off beyond the barren plains.

He awoke sweating and shivering.

'What is it Giorgio?' his wife mumbled beside him.

'We have to go home,' he announced grimly.

* * *

THEY ARRIVED BACK the following morning to find the party still in progress. Intoxicated revellers lay in heaps across the driveway, on the patio and throughout the house, much like the dead at Isandlwana. The garden furniture bobbed in the pool. Inside the house the carpets were speckled with cigarette burns, and the living room suite was dappled with food stains, spilled drink and splashes of vomit. Each bedroom housed the slumbering aftermath of Caligulan orgies.

In stunned silence Giorgio went from room to room, following the stinging pungency of burning paper. The trail led him to his shed.

The doors had been forced, the contents ransacked. A single stoned reveller lay beneath his workbench. On the shelves his blackened notebooks still smouldered. Giorgio staggered from the scene of destruction, his face pale.

'My kingdom has fallen,' he whispered.

* * *

AFTER THE DISASTER, friends and family rallied round to help them paper over the cracks in time for the end-of-summer party. But Giorgio was a changed man. He no longer spoke in anything other than scientific or philosophical riddles and word spread that his mind was broken.

While others repainted walls and replaced carpets, he repaired his shed and spent more and more time there. Day and night the songs of the hammer and saw were punctuated with flashes of arc welding. Giorgio would emerge at dawn, pale

122

and drawn, to sleep a few hours before once more returning to his Vulcan labours.

Although his family were somewhat concerned, they presumed that he would snap out of his malaise sooner or later, and besides they had more than sufficient troubles of their own to deal with! As the day of the end-of-summer party approached, preparations continued and stress levels rose. In the midst of all this, Giorgio's behaviour became, if anything, stranger. But for the most part those around him were too preoccupied to notice.

One day, child number six asked her mother about it. 'Mum, have you seen Papa lately?'

'Yes, of course I have,' her mother replied. She was discussing seating arrangements with a representative from the caterers and deliberating over which hors d'oeuvres to serve.

'How long's he been wearing an eyepatch?' child six said.

'An eyepatch?' her mother repeated, looking up. 'Oh I don't know. The eyepatch is a new one on me.'

'And that dress, the one with the moons and stars all over it?'

'It's not a dress, dear. It's a robe,' her mother corrected. 'There's a difference. And, anyway, aren't there little suns on it too?'

'I think so,' her daughter said, frowning hard as she tried to recall.

'Well then, that's the same dress, I mean *robe*, that he's been wearing for the past couple of weeks.'

'Oh, right. Hadn't noticed until now,' child six said. 'And what about the winged sandals? Are they new?'

'Winged sandals?' her mother replied in surprise. 'Look, I'm awful busy here. Could we talk more about this later?'

* * *

ON THE DAY of the party the skies were clear and the air perfectly dry and warm. Taxis passed up and down the drive like a stream of metal beetles, disgorging their cargoes to be greeted by Giorgio's wife and daughters. The guests were welcomed, handed glasses of dry, well-chilled cava and thereafter sent to gather in the garden about the pool. There they sipped their drinks and engaged in murmured conversation.

To the rear of the garden, where an arched double gate led out towards the farms and hills, a great shape towered. It was easily twelve feet high and draped in an expansive shroud of white cloth. At first the mystery object elicited a good deal of conversation. As the cava flowed, however, talk turned to more everyday matters and the obtrusive presence was filtered out, much like the dinosaurs one sometimes encounters in the lounges of private homes, which those living there collude fiercely to deny.

Time passed. Shadows stretched across the land. The sky cycled through the palette of sunset, thereafter deepening from azure, to lapis lazuli and finally into night. Stars appeared. Giorgio emerged from his shed and passed quietly among the guests, greeting them and commenting on proceedings as only he could. In return the guests smiled warmly, and if they were surprised at his appearance they did their utmost not to let it show.

'Hello, Giorgio. How are you?'

Giorgio turned to regard the speaker, sequins on his black leather eyepatch reflecting starlight.

'I am much as Merlin was when he vanished from the world of humankind,' he replied, fingering a quail's egg-sized multi-faceted jewel that dangled at his throat.

'Er, yes, of course.'

And he moved on through the assembly, leaving little groups of revellers to gather closer, their heads together.

'Terrible shame . . .' they whispered.

'Yes, quite mad, quite mad.'

Giorgio was neither deceived by the visitors nor vexed by them.

'The entangled forest is my domain,' he told a corpulent woman and her entourage of friends. 'And my movements are those of wind and breath.'

'Yes, and that's an awfully nice kaftan you're wearing, Giorgio,' the woman said with a smile that convinced nobody.

'What? This old rag? Giorgio answered with a shrug. 'I find it comfortable, and by the way it's a robe.'

'A robe,' the woman agreed, nodding furiously, her grin so fiercely fixed it brought on cramp in her lower jaw and dimpled cheeks.

'And while we're on the subject,' he announced, 'my heart has grown as light as a feather.'

'A feather, of course.'

He gave a dignified nod then and, with a wave of his hand, vanished into the press.

'Oh dear, his poor, poor wife,' they murmured behind his back.

When the call came for everyone to be seated, Giorgio had disappeared. And while nobody commented on the fact, those who had spoken to him felt it was probably for the best.

Giorgio's wife bid everyone welcome once more and, raising their glasses to the summer season now officially at a close, they began on their starters. Soft music filtered up from the quadrophonic sound system that Giorgio has constructed from scavenged components several summers previously.

All seemed well.

After the starter, new wines were poured and the evening's main course was served. More toasts were made and the guests' glasses were raised all the more frequently. Conversation heavily laced with laughter rose up to the heavens. After dessert had been cleared away and coffee was brewing, one of the guests got to his feet to speak a few words of thanks. He tapped his glass with a knife and waited patiently as the assembly grew quiet. Then he opened his mouth.

At that precise moment a battery of spotlights cleverly concealed among the rosebushes erupted into light. Their beams arced and rotated for a time, before converging onto the shrouded mystery object. Next a great drum roll boomed around the garden and echoed off over the surrounding land. In its wake a dispersed chorus of barking, bleating and other panicked animal cries rose up in sympathy.

The guests sat in stunned silence.

A countdown commenced in a deep male voice with an American accent. 'Ten, nine, eight . . .'

Frozen where they sat, the guests' faces betrayed increasing trepidation and perplexity.

'Oh dear,' Giorgio's wife hissed to child number six.

'What is it, mum?'

'I think your dad's done something to the sound system.'

'. . . three, two, one, *ignition* . . .'

The strains of Strauss's *Thus Spake Zarathustra* exploded over the speakers at such a volume that many instinctively clapped hands to their ears, while their full bellies quaked to the drums' infrasound percussions. The shroud slipped to the ground in rippling folds and a collective gasp sounded as the mystery was revealed.

Before them stood a great figure wrapped in metal. It glittered coldly, its form human, yet so encased in chains it might have been a monument to Houdini.

The music rose to a climactic crescendo and a mass of small explosions swept across the figure, eliciting shrieks of fear and alarm. The chains fell away in a cascade of shattered steel links and, beneath them, a shining, metallic angel was revealed, rearing over the garden. Many of the guests had by now risen to their feet. Some were backing slowly away.

To the drone of hidden servos, two vast wings unfolded from the angel's back and began flapping in great slow sweeps. Smoke and flames spewed and guttered from its feet as booster rockets ignited and thrust hard to raise it slowly, slowly above scorched and smouldering rose beds.

'*We have lift off!*'

In a garden now increasingly fogged by smoke, cries of alarm were being replaced by ragged applause.

Giorgio spoke:

'Some of us believe we seek freedom,' his voice said from the speakers. 'Yet from the earliest times we are enslaved. Dramas of fate and the web of those with whom we are surrounded enmesh us in ever deeper bonds. Our desires and fears encircle us and lead us onto lesser paths. We are governed by pettiness and the tactics of hiding.

'Behold, I have taken flight! I have shed shackles and burned bridges. More, I have burned my garden! I have transcended to become that which the gods want of me and now I move in the infinite, the riddle of my soul reflected back at me from all I see!'

And with that, the great wings beat harder and he soared up into the starry vastness, there among the terrors of the boundless to embrace liberation.

* * *

In Castalla, though years have passed, they speak of the old man still. And sometimes by night, his call can be heard as he rides the cosmic winds, but there are few, if any, who can understand it.

The Golem

Caimh McDonnell

IN A DUSTY AND CAREWORN ROOM, AN EMACIATED MAN WEEPS.
He isn't aware of his own tears. His mind is elsewhere. His face is a
mask of pained concentration – eyes shut tightly, teeth clenched. He sits
in a large armchair, his frail body lost in a vastly over-sized t-shirt that envelops his
frail form. You couldn't be blamed for looking at him and thinking that it might
be kinder if whatever was killing him would just hurry up and finish the job.

In a brief moment of respite, his eyelids open, to reveal two gaping holes where
eyeballs should be. He looks up at a ceiling that he cannot see. His spindly hand
uses the corner of his t-shirt sleeve to dab at tears of blood on his face.

Another wave hits and his pain-filled vigil resumes.

* * *

FRANK TOOK OUT his rag and carefully cleaned the already spotless glass.

'If you're not careful, you're going to wear a hole in it.'

His face reddened as he turned and saw his niece Gina beaming at him from
behind the counter. 'I'm paying you to make pizza, not laugh at me.'

'I know, Uncle Frank. I consider it my bonus.'

He playfully tossed the rag at her, but Gina ducked and giggled, avoiding it
with ease. 'I'll make up some boxes and let you get back to admiring your view.'

'Yeah, you do that.'

Frank stepped back and looked through the window; he did, he really did – he
had a view. Not much of one, sure, but a view nonetheless. The Falls had been
his home since he was a boy so he knew all too well that it was nobody's idea of

a tourist attraction. In fact, until recently – if anybody from out-of-town was unlucky enough to stumble into this neighbourhood – they were in for the worst and possibly last day of their lives.

It hadn't always been like that. Sure, in his childhood it had been no Eden, but it had been a community. Most people had had work and, more importantly, pride. You might be struggling to make the rent, but the stoop outside your house was still going to gleam. Your body might've ached from hard manual labor but you still took the trash out on a Thursday and cleaned the windows.

And then, the trade from the docks had moved down the coast and taken the jobs with it. Those who were smart got out and took their pride with them. In came the drugs, the gangs, the whores and worse. At some point, what had been a working class neighborhood became a ghetto and the gleaming windows got replaced with battered chipboard. At his aunt's pleading, Frank had taken over the place after uncle Tony had been stabbed by a junkie for the 23 bucks in the cash register. Tony had retired upstate, his farewell gifts being the steel mesh over the windows and the loaded shotgun under the counter.

That had been twelve years ago and The Falls had only sunk deeper and deeper into the mire. Politicians and promises had come and gone. Soon the darkness of the night had encroached further and further into the day, as the sickness had spread and the whole body had become infected. It hadn't been long before not even the daylight offered protection. The police now always had somewhere else to be. The Falls had become lost, and lost all hope with it. That was until he had come.

Frank noticed old Mrs. Granger across the street, out walking that yappy little dog of hers, and waved. She waved back. Imagine that, an old lady bringing her dog out for an evening stroll in The Falls. He couldn't help but shake his head in wonder. How times had changed.

'Is that him?!' Gina squealed excitedly as she rushed to the window. Frank snapped out of his reverie and looked where she was pointing. There he stood, on the roof of the Brownstone opposite. He'd been referred to by many names: The Angel, The Guardian of The Falls, and so on. People needed heroes. The name that had stuck though had been the Golem.

Gina had never seen him before. Frank had only allowed her to come work for him a few weeks ago when things had become safer.

'Yeah that's him,' he said.

'Oh.' Gina sounded disappointed. 'I was expecting somebody, I dunno . . . bigger.'

She had a point. The Golem didn't look all that. He was the size of a well-built man of average-to-stocky frame, blond-haired and wearing a battered pair of patched and ill-fitting overalls. Not exactly what the comic books would lead you to expect, he looked more the wholesome farm-boy type than anything otherworldly.

It was only when you got closer that you sensed it. First you'd notice the weird vacant smile – like he was a little bit spaced out. Stoned, but not. It was like you were part of his bad trip. He never spoke, never even made a sound – just walked silently, like a ghost amongst men. What made it real were those eyes. Frank had seen them up close a couple of times – ice-blue and piercing.

'Although, he is kinda cute,' said Gina. 'Do you think he has a girlfriend?'

Frank snapped at her more than he had meant: 'Never you mind, young lady! Get back to work. You leave that man well enough alone, you hear me?'

He saw the wounded look in her eyes and instantly knew he'd gone too far. 'I didn't – I mean . . .'

She turned and walked quickly around the counter and off into the back. Frank felt like a Grade A asshole. He'd apologise later – maybe let her go home early.

He turned back in time to see the Golem casually step off the roof and drop five floors to the alley below.

If an ordinary man survived that fall at all, he'd probably wish he hadn't, being broken seven ways from Sunday. The Golem landed unnaturally – like he had no bones at all within his body, as if he'd just stepped off the kerb. It seemed like gravity didn't dictate to him, but that he'd play along with it if he felt like it. Those piercing blue eyes turned towards Frank, and he started as an involuntary shiver shimmied down his spine. He reddened and looked away, before thinking better of it and waving nervously. He didn't want to appear ungrateful.

Then, Frank turned away and started fussing about with the napkins on the counter.

A minute later, the bell over the shop door tinkled and Frank turned to see Father Pat beaming at him from the doorway. 'Do these old eyes deceive me or does somebody have a window?'

Frank couldn't help but grin. 'Installed fresh this morning, Father.'

Father Pat stepped into the shop and theatrically gave the window an appraising look. 'Well now, ain't she a thing of beauty?'

You couldn't help but like the old priest; seventy if he was a day and possessed of a distinctive Irish lilt despite having never left the state in his whole life. These days, he was more like the man Frank remembered from his youth – quick to laugh, a glint in his eye and the kind of lively spirit that could get a smile out of even the surliest of teenagers. Frank loved to see him like this. Back in the dark days, he'd maybe gone from liking a drink to needing it and the glint had been dulled.

Today the old man was positively beaming. 'I've just been around to meet that new couple that moved in down the block. As sweet as pie and they've a little angel with them. We're going to be having a christening a week on Saturday!'

'That's wonderful.'

It was too. Frank couldn't remember the last time somebody had actually moved *to* The Falls. It wasn't somewhere you moved to, it was somewhere you ended up when hope, money and the will to fight had left you.

'You should see their building as well,' continued Father Pat, 'looking mighty nice, almost back to its old self.' A silent moment passed between the two men as they shared a memory they'd both rather forget. That had been Leon's building. He'd been a security guard, and a good man, even if his temper had blown a little hot at times. That's what had done for him in the end. He'd been crazy enough to stand up to The Skulls after one of their little joyrides had left his son in the hospital. He'd given them a piece of his mind.

They'd hung Leon's battered body off the roof so everybody could see. It'd been there for a day and a night before the fire brigade had been willing to come in with a heavy police escort to cut it down.

* * *

FATHER PAT SNAPPED back to the present as Gina emerged from the kitchen. 'And who, pray tell, is this vision of loveliness?'

It was Gina's turn to look a little embarrassed. 'This is my niece Gina, Father. She's been kind enough to come help out her poor uncle. She's been doing a stellar job.'

Gina smiled shyly – an acknowledgement that the harsh words of earlier had been forgotten. Father Pat bowed theatrically. 'Charmed to make your acquaintance, m'lady. I hope this reprobate isn't being too much of an ogre to work for?'

Gina grinned again. 'Oh, he has his moments.'

'Gina is my sister Carol's youngest.'

Father Pat clapped his hands with delight. 'Of course! Do tell her I was asking after her.'

'Sure thing. Now, what can I get you?'

Father Pat stepped back and perused the menu above the counter with great ceremony. 'I will have . . . an Americana with cheese, please, my dear.'

'Great. That'll be–'

Frank cut across her. 'Oh, no. The Padre's money is no good here.'

Pat made a face and pulled out his wallet. 'Don't be silly, Francis. Are we going have to have this fight every time I come in here?'

'Only until you give in and just accept it.'

'Oh, you're a terrible man.'

'That's why I need God on my side. If you like, you can shave off a few Hail Marys from my penance next week.'

Father Pat slipped his wallet back into his pocket. 'Ahhh, there ain't nothing in this life for free.'

Gina slipped a pie into the pizza oven and then walloped the door to get it to close. Father Pat looked up with a start.

'Yeah, I've a new oven coming next month,' said Frank, 'and I'm thinking of getting some tables and chairs for outside too. Y'know, for the summer.'

'Well I'll be. Al fresco dining in the Falls. Who'd a thunk it?' said Father Pat. 'And how're you affording all this expansion?'

'Well, now I don't have to pay protection anymore, this place is finally making some money . . .'

'Thanks be to God.'

'. . . and the Whale,' interjected Gina.

Father Pat looked confused and Frank cursed his big mouth. He should never have said anything to Gina, but she'd kept on asking. She'd wanted to know where he kept disappearing to every day.

'The Whale' as Gina had dubbed him was Frank's best customer. Hell, back in the bad old days, him moving into the neighborhood had singlehandedly kept the business afloat. Well, that and the fact that the bank didn't want to foreclose on a property nobody in their right mind would want to buy.

He was a shut-in over on Broadhurst. A nice enough guy, once you got used to the look of him and the . . . well, Frank hated to admit it but the guy really stank.

He'd moved back in to his Grandma's place when she'd died and, as far as Frank could tell, he hadn't left since. He'd apparently lived there as a child, but there'd been some trouble and he'd been sent away. It was nothing terrible, as Frank understood it. He was maybe just an odd kid – he sure was an odd adult.

Every day, he ordered a dozen pies, a bucket load of sides and three quarts of soda, and he paid in cash, plus a big tip for delivery. It had been the only delivery Frank would make back in the dark days – that good a customer was worth the risk. The guy must've weighed 500 pounds easy, and Frank couldn't help but feel bad about it. He'd made the mistake of telling Carol and she'd said he was something Oprah called 'an enabler'. Was it Frank's business how someone chose to live their life? If he didn't make the delivery, somebody else would. He'd never mentioned it to Father Pat though, not even in confession. You can't confess a sin if you know you're going to be committing it again tomorrow and the next day. Gina was like her mother – she could never keep a secret either. Frank needed a change of subject, and luckily one occurred to him.

'Did you hear?' said Frank, looking out the window. 'Jimmy has been onto the city council again, and he says they're definitely coming out next week to fix the streetlights.'

'That's fantastic news because . . .' Father Pat tailed off, noticing Frank's distraction.

Frank stared, a feeling of dread building inside him. Sometimes in life, you can see exactly what's going to happen, but you're powerless to stop it – like a car crash on an icy road. When the skid starts and the vehicle goes from under you, all you can do is watch with that sinking feeling in your stomach. That was what it was like now.

A car had pulled up across the street and a kid not much older than Gina was getting out. The driver looked older, like maybe he was the brains of the outfit – everything is relative. The kid wore a jacket that was too heavy for the weather and a look on his face that Frank had seen before. That pissed off at the world look that a nervous person gets when they've fired themselves up to do something. Add in that junkie twitch, and this kid was only going to be bad news. Frank would've reacted sooner back in the old days, but he'd stopped expecting trouble around every corner. This trouble though was walking right in the front door.

Father Pat was turning his head to look, as the bell above the door tinkled and the kid was already half through, pulling the gun Frank had known would be there. He held it a foot from the old priest's head and scanned the room anxiously.

'Nobody fucking move, you hear me?'

Frank looked to see Gina frozen in horror behind the counter. On her first day he'd told her – first sign of trouble, get down, stay down, no matter what. Now that the moment had arrived, she'd frozen like a rabbit in the headlights.

'OK, son,' said Frank. 'Just take it easy.'

That got the gun turned on him for his trouble. 'I ain't your fucking son, motherfucker.'

Frank raised his hands slowly to show he meant no harm. The kid's eyes darted to Gina. 'Gimme the register, bitch. All of it.'

Somewhere inside, scared as she was, Gina was still her mother's daughter. That was a great thing in Frank's eyes almost all the time, but not now. 'I ain't a bitch.'

'What did you say . . . bitch?'

Frank moved fast to stay in front of the gun as it swung around to point at her. 'She said nothing. Gina, give the man what's in the register.'

'But–'

'Now!' The sharpness in his tone and the pleading look in his eyes made her start doing as he asked. She opened the drawer and began placing the money on the counter.

Father Pat spoke in a near whisper. 'Do you know where you are, lad? This is The Falls.'

'What do I care where the hell I am?'

Frank was surprised when the next person that spoke turned out to be him. 'Oh God. You don't know. You're from out of town, aren't you?'

The kid's eyes widened at this, confusion and panic threatening to overwhelm him. This in turn scared Frank – a frightened man with a gun is capable of anything.

'Just take the money and–'

The kid cracked Frank above the ear with the handle of the gun and grabbed for the money on the counter.

'UNCLE FRANK!'

Frank's knees buckled, but Father Pat grabbed him under the arm. The old man was deceptively strong for one so slight.

The kid dropped some of the money as he rushed for the door, but he kept on running. Coins tinkled all around on the tiled floor.

They watched him dive into the backseat of the waiting car. The tyres raised smoke as it sped away. Gina rushed around the counter and knelt down beside Frank.

Then there was a moment of stillness. Gina looked at Frank, but Frank and Father Pat only stared out the window at the now empty street.

'Maybe he's not watching,' said Father Pat.

Frank put his hand to the side of his head to feel for blood. 'He's always watching.'

* * *

THE CAR MADE it all of thirty yards before it coming to a juddering halt. The Golem had fallen from the sky and landed on the bonnet – crushing the front of the vehicle in a cacophony of tortured machinery. The driver didn't get much of a chance to consider the utter impossibility of a man doing that to a couple of tonnes of metal. He can't have been wearing a seatbelt because he came hurtling out through the front window. The Golem calmly extended his right hand and caught him like he was fielding a frisbee tossed by an eight-year-old. The last thing the driver saw was the Golem looking at him with those piercing blue eyes and that vacant grin on his face.

'What the f–'

The Golem ripped him clean in half – lengthways. It was like he was just tearing through tissue paper. The front of his overalls and his face were now covered in blood and God knows what else. Still that smile remained fixed in place.

Meanwhile, the kid with the gun had made it out. He was limping badly, blood staining the front left thigh of his jeans as he dragged a gimpy leg with every ounce of energy he had.

'C'mon, kid, move!' said Frank. 'Before . . .'

* * *

The kid stopped as something landed in front of him. Frank craned to make out what it was, and then wished he hadn't. It was the driver's head, still with half a spinal cord attached.

The kid turned to see The Golem standing behind him, that eerily calm grin on his face, as if the blood was just a light shower of rain he'd been caught in. The eyes were the worst part, thought Frank. It wasn't the anger; it was the joy.

The kid drew his gun and the Golem danced as half a dozen bullets ripped into his torso. They entered him but never left. He didn't flinch or stumble. The Golem's overalls would need some more patches, but even now Frank could see the flesh reforming around what you could hardly call a wound. It was like shooting sand.

The kid looked in bewilderment at his gun, then at the Golem, then back to the gun. Frank's stomach turned as he watched the Golem's slow advance. He wished the poor fool would just run, while at the same time he knew it would be utterly pointless. Instead, the kid dropped to his knees and started begging for his life. The Golem stood above him and calmly looked down as he pleaded his case.

He reached out his left hand and softly stroked the boy's face, an incongruous act that, if judged in isolation, would look loving veering towards sensuous. Then with his right hand he lightly tapped him on the other cheek. Frank didn't need to see the boy's eyes to know that suddenly there would be hope there amidst the terror and confusion.

Then the Golem's left hand slapped his cheek almost playfully…

Then the right, a little harder…

Frank looked down at the floor, unable to watch. He'd seen Carol's cat do this with a mouse once. Father Pat similarly looked away, mumbling softly to ease his conscience. 'Somebody should do something.'

Maybe somebody should, but Frank looked into his soul and knew it wouldn't be him. Even if he'd wanted to, what good would it do? And while he might end up tossing and turning at night, haunted by the memory, he knew deep down he didn't *want* to do anything. He wished things were different, but he also remembered what it had been like before.

There ain't nothing in this life for free.

Frank must've been lost in his own thoughts, desperate to block out the sight of the kid's hands uselessly trying to fend off the blows as the Golem built towards a crescendo. That could be the only explanation for why he'd not heard the bell over the door.

'STOP IT!'

Frank looked up just in time to see Gina grab at the Golem's right arm as she rushed towards him. She collided with his backswing and was tossed back through the air maybe ten feet, slamming into the side of a parked Buick.

The Golem stopped and turned his head towards Gina.

Time slowed to a crawl. Frank's feet carried him out to the street while his mind filled with memories of the past and visions of the future. Carol with her beautiful new baby in her arms – joy, pride, terror and exhaustion mixed together in a new mother's smile. Gina's first communion, the look of feisty tomboy indignation in her eyes, daring the world to tell her she looked pretty. Then the conversation with Carol to explain what'd happened. He could hear his own hollow words echoing back to him, his meaningless platitudes of sorrow for the loss of her sweet innocent daughter.

And then – finally – he was there, standing between the two of them. Those cold blue eyes stared right at him.

'Please . . . she didn't mean it. She doesn't understand.'

Gina cradled her broken arm against her as she slowly and painfully propped herself against the car and then began to push herself to her feet.

'I understand fine. He's a monster.'

'She doesn't–'

'I do!' Her voice was stronger now, as she looked straight into the Golem's eyes. 'You're a monster. You don't have the right to . . . You're not God!'

Frank held his breath as the Golem looked at Gina, then down into the poor pathetic face of the kid. Frank looked down at him too. Even amongst all the blood and swollen flesh you couldn't help but see he was, after all, just a kid. The fear and incomprehension were there, but more cruelly hope. He stared up into the Golem's cold eyes and every inch of his being pleaded for mercy. He looked upwards as if to a saviour, forgetting what he was looking to be saved from.

The Golem turned to Gina, a look in his eyes that may have said a lot but none of it in a language Frank could understand. As their eyes met, they held the moment for what felt like the longest time. Gina was transfixed, so much so that she didn't realise that the casual flick of the Golem's wrist was him breaking the kid's neck.

And with a casual step, the Golem leapt the top of the brownstone building. As Gina's scream reverberated around the neighborhood.

Frank thought that the look in her eyes as she'd watched the Golem leave was the worst thing he'd ever seen. Then she looked at him and he realised he'd been wrong.

* * *

In a dusty and careworn room, an emaciated man weeps.

He stops his slow rocking back and forth as the figure of the Golem towers over him. The Golem looks down at the frail figure, extends his hand and they touch. The weeping man's spindly hand looks so frail as it rests in the other's large, blood-stained fingers.

The frail man grows and the Golem shrinks away, until in a matter of minutes both have disappeared. They're replaced by the morbidly obese frame of a 500-pound man, who is stretching the t-shirt he wears to its absolute limit and beyond.

His piercing blue eyes stare up at the ceiling and he sighs deeply. He is the kind of tired that never goes away.

Ain't nothing in this life for free.

The Angel in Ida Tueboll's Cupboard

Matthew White

About Ida Tueboll

ONCE THERE WAS A GIRL WHO MADE THINGS HAPPEN, AND THAT GIRL WAS named Ida Tueboll. If a child cried, it was because Ida Tueboll made them cry. If a dog ran away, it was running from Ida Tueboll. If a building collapsed . . . well, eyebrows were raised.

Ida Tueboll was 14, and she still wore child-sized shoes. And yet there were 18-year-old knife-wielding club bouncers on her street who were terrified of Ida Tueboll.

Ida Tueboll could deliver a swift moment of terror, or a year-long campaign of mental disintegration. She could topple the coolest clique, and she could dismantle the tough-guy gangs if she so choose.

She could put her mind to anything, and for most of her life she had put her mind to being a bully. And that was why Ida Tueboll was the scariest girl in the city.

Ida Tueboll Draws the Important Shapes

First came the circle: it had to be exactly nine feet in diameter, and utterly perfect. This did not daunt Ida Tueboll: she had spent a week constructing the perfect pair of compasses from her Dad's favourite pool cue.

Then, inside the circle, there was the pentangle. To get this just right Ida Tueboll used a wooden frame, carefully constructed from her little Brother's cot.

And then she had to write the 72 sacred names of the God around the outside of the circle. This was the tricky bit.

To get the 72 names right Ida Tueboll had taken her Mother's favourite torch, and she had rigged it up to a frame – also made from the cot – and she had shone the torch through a print-out of the names, and everything was so perfectly placed that she only had to trace over the shadows of the names in chalk to get things just right.

And they had to be right – the 72 names were one of the most important building blocks of the ritual. She concentrated so hard she forgot all about the annoying sniffle that had been building in her head the last couple of days.

Finally the 72 names were traced, and Ida Tueboll stepped back carefully to survey her work. This flimsy chalk diagram of circle and pentagram and names was one part of a construction that would stop her from being torn apart. The second half, the triangle, was the trap in which her target would be caught and forced to do the bidding of Ida Tueboll.

So Ida Tueboll drew the triangle exactly seven feet from the circle, using angles and lines carefully worked out, and guided by more frames made from cots, table legs and a guitar neck she reasoned that her Dad would not miss.

It was tiring work, and bending over for so long was back-breaking, so Ida Tueboll was quite pleased with herself when she saw how splendid the finished work looked.

And then she sneezed, and it didn't look quite so splendid anymore.

When Ida Tueboll had completed her work for the second time, she was in no mood to carry out the ritual that night, and she went to bed and fell into a deep sleep.

Ida Tueboll never lay awake or worried about things. That sort of thing was for weak people, and Ida was never more certain that she was strong.

Ida Tueboll Makes an Angel of Her Own.

The next morning Ida Tueboll set to work. She drew her curtains, read through the ritual one more time and chanted it under her breath. The cold had developed overnight, and she now had a tickle in her throat too. Ida Tueboll was strong, but she was not stupid, so she made sure that she had plenty of water before she began.

And begin she did – calling the names of all the spirits that would protect her from the spirit she was trying to conjure. She wrapped her tongue around the strange pronunciation: Ida Tueboll was 14, and she should have failed all of her studies (she did not because Ida Tueboll was very studious when it came to blackmail), but she could work hard when she wanted, and now she knew 72 ancient Middle eastern names off by heart.

The ritual went on and on, hour after hour of pleas, threats and compliments. Ida Tueboll's concentration was total – and there was no chance that her Parents would disturb her. They had tried that once when she was seven, and it had taken them a week to get over the shock.

After she had called out the 72 sacred names, and dealt with each of them individually, Ida Tueboll then had to use the right words to call the spirit to her room. This had been the hardest part of the ritual to set out – it didn't seem that many people had tried to bring a Ljósálfr into the here and now.

The hardest part was the mix of languages. Arabic here, English there. Norwegian over here. But Ida Tueboll had never let something like that get in her way, and she had spent weeks studying the ancient texts, and finding the right combination of ancient words of power and modern words of convenience, so that when the time came she was confident that she would be successful.

And so it was a shame that, after all of her work, she forgot to take a final sip of water, just as she entered into the final sentence of the thousands that the ritual required.

She coughed, and so when she was supposed to say:

'And by the holy branch of the mistletoe I call you, Ljósálfr, to my realm!'

What she actually said was something like:

'And by the holy branch of the mistletoe I call you eaarrgh splurgle gurgle eresh ki gaaaal, sorry, Ljósálfr, to my realm!'

Ida Tueboll cursed silently, gulped the water, and waited.

Ida Tueboll was strong, but not too strong to deny fear. She knew the rules – she knew how important names were when conjuring, and she knew that she could, inadvertently, have called something horrible to this world. Something called 'Eaarrgh splurgle gurgle'!

She stopped talking to herself, and peered into the shaded triangle.

There was nothing there, but she could feel a change in the atmosphere of the room. It was cold, which meant nothing. Cold was normal for this situation. But she was soon glad of the water, as she found her mouth becoming dry, drier than her Mum's Brunost on toast.

The entire room was turning into a desert. And Ida Tueboll was sure she could hear something, away in the distance . . . a faint tinkling of bells.

Ida Tueboll suppressed a shiver, and she looked again. A moment before there had been nothing, and now there was something.

Ida Tueboll squinted and peered, for whatever was inside the triangle was hard to make out. She could see a cold light hovering inches above the wooden floor. The light increased in intensity until, a metre above the wood, it was almost blinding.

Ida Tueboll covered her eyes and tried to speak, but her mouth was too dry until she had taken another sip of water.

And finally she was able to blurt out the question:

'Are you a servant of the Light?'

Ida Tueboll Talks to Her Angel

Silence. The light hovered, and Ida Tueboll knew that she had to take command of the situation.

'I order you to respond. Are you a servant of the Light?'

This was unusual for Ida Tueboll – normally people would do as she said, but then they knew that failure to comply would usually end with some complex revenge, perhaps involving a bucket of pig's blood or a dangerous stick.

But she was still aware of the gravity of the situation, so Ida Tueboll proceeded slowly.

'Are you . . .'

'Yes.'

The voice came from the middle of the light, and it came from the walls and the ceiling and from inside her head. Ida Tueboll gasped, thrilled and a shivered. For a moment Ida Tueboll was thrown by the sheer magnitude of her actions. But she quickly mastered herself, and tried to adopt her most confident voice as she launched into her prepared speech.

'I called you to this plane of existence to do my bidding. And now you will do my bidding.'

The light bobbed . . . more silence.

'And you will now do my bidding, or I will condemn you to an eternity of . . .'

Ida Tueboll hesitated, and faltered slightly as she tried to remember the rest of the line. She knew that it was something about pain and suffering, but it would not come. So she improvised.

'I will condemn you to an eternity of being my enemy. And no-one wants to be my enemy. I summoned you here to be my guardian Angel. Do you understand?'

There was no answer. But Ida Tueboll was not deterred.

'Do you understand? Do you understand? Do you understand?'

And after two hours of Ida Tueboll asking the question, the light spoke.

'I am no Angel.'

'Angels are weak. I called upon a Ljósálfr, and you will act as my guardian Angel and do everything a guardian Angel should do.'

There was a slight delay, the cold intensified and dryness began to eat at Ida Tueboll's skin. And then the voice spoke once more.

'Until when?'

'Until I am done with you.'

'There will be a payment.'

Ida Tueboll had expected this. It was in the Second Appendix to The Weird Book of Folk Tales, which was called: 'Bringing Spirits into Our Plane (Based On Works By Aleister Crowley)'. In fact, all of the instructions Ida Tueboll had followed were in this book.

'Name your price.'

And the light spoke instantly.

'You will accompany me to my homeland.'

Ida Tueboll pondered for a moment. She knew all about Álfheimr, home of the Light Elves.

'Forever?'

'For all time.'

Ida Tueboll stifled a gasp, but the light spoke once more.

'Or until you tire of my homeland and leave us.'

The Second Appendix to the Weird Book of Folk Tales was very clear on dealing with the Spirit you have brought into Our Plane. And its advice was:

'Do not accept anything. Do not bargain. Ever.'

But Ida Tueboll was becoming impatient, and part of her really wanted to see Álfheimr. And the offer was quite clear: she could leave whenever she wanted.

'I accept your offer.'

Which was the first mistake Ida Tueboll made. But she did not know this yet. Instead she watched the light dim slightly, and smiled when that voice was everywhere once more.

'Name your desire.'

Ida Tueboll leaned forward in her circle of safety.

'Make me nice.'

More about Ida Tueboll

No one knew what made Ida Tueboll want to be nice, apart from Ida Tueboll. There were those who said that the truth was hidden in the vile story 'The Nine Rules of the Nisse', written by the Mad Arab Matthew White. But Ida Tueboll was not about to confirm or deny those rumours.

She never lived in the past, and all that was important was that she wanted to be nice. And if Ida Tueboll wanted to be nice, then of course she was going to be the nicest person in the country.

But she had not found it easy. Ida Tueboll never lived in the past, but her schoolmates did. So when she smiled at them they got scared. They all knew that this could perfectly well be the first phase of a new, ambitious reign of horror.

And when she brought them treats they threw them away and washed their hands until they were raw. And when she spoke to them they screamed and ran. And when she didn't cover them with pig's blood . . . they waited for her to cover them in pig's blood.

Things came to a head when the School Psychologist called Ida Tueboll into her office to ask – quietly, tremulously – what Ida Tueboll was doing. And when Ida Tueboll explained that she was trying to be nice, the School Psychologist had laughed – for a second.

And when Ida Tueboll pulled a face, and she saw how this made the School Psychologist stop laughing and whimper a little bit, she realised that she would need supernatural help in her quest to be nice.

Ida Tueboll Argues with Her Guardian Angel

Ida Tueboll had expected a more immediate response from the Ljósálfr. Being nice was their kind of thing, their speciality. But the light just hovered in her bedroom, silent and dry and cold.

'Spirit! You must do my bidding.'

There was silence. Ida Tueboll prepared to threaten the spirit again, but finally it spoke.

'I am thinking.'

And so Ida Tueboll left her Angel to think. She had expected that the creature would be in her room for some time – even Ljósálfr cannot work miracles overnight – and so she had rigged her bedroom cupboard for this eventuality.

She had removed its base, and suspended it directly over the triangle, using a block and tackle mechanism her Dad had built for her under threat of violence.

Being good was not easy.

So she carefully lowered the cupboard over the light, and she surrounded the triangle with extra protection, and she left the Ljósálfr to think whilst she had a good night's sleep.

The next day Ida Tueboll left the cupboard closed, as she wanted the Ljósálfr to get its answer just right. She was not going to go through all of this for nothing.

The day was a trial. She tried to be nice at every turn, but she just could not do it. For a moment she considered returning to her bad old ways – just a tennis ball to the face or an 'accident' involving rope in the gym – but she held her nerve.

She had commissioned a Ljósálfr to make her good, and it had better be worth it.

But when she returned to her room she was not pleased with the response.

'Why do you need an Angel to make you nice? Can you not exercise your Human will?'

Ida Tueboll seethed a little. And she spoke very quietly.

'You waited for nearly twenty hours to say that?'

'I am a . . . an Angel. My passage of time is not your passage of time.'

Ida Tueboll pondered for a moment, the light in her cupboard pulsing gently, as though it were the only thing in the room. Then she ran from the house.

Within an hour she was sitting, alone, in the library, her nose deep in the Book of Weird Folk Tales. She had been reading for no more than a couple of minutes before she was throwing the book into the hands of the stupefied Librarian and running back home.

When she got home she ran into the living room, where her family was enjoying a nice quiet night in by the fire. She grabbed the wrought iron poker from the companion set and sprinted upstairs to her room.

There she flung the cupboard door open and, without a moment's hesitation, she rammed the point of the poker into the light. There was a CRACK, and the light wavered, and the voice that was everywhere cried out in pain.

Ida Tueboll retreated into her pentangle and waited whilst the Ljósálfr threw curses at her, the light dancing and jumping and flaring.

'You whelping bitch! You hyena, you eater of fouled meat! You dare to strike at me! I, who have commanded my land for longer than you pathetic sub-creatures have crawled through your stinking dung!'

Eventually the curses subsided and, when the light was silent, Ida Tueboll spoke again.

'Next time I'll heat the iron in the fire, and I'll work out where your anus is before I shove it in.'

The light stopped flaring.

'You would not dare!'

Ida Tueboll did not answer, but her expression spoke volumes.

'You would dare.'

Ida Tueboll nodded.

'Now – you have until I wake up tomorrow. Make me nice.'

And she shut the door on the Ljósálfr and went to sleep.

Ida Tueboll never dreamt. So in her mind she closed her eyes, and within a moment she opened them again, and she knew that it was daytime, and hours had passed.

She opened the cupboard and stared at the light. And the Ljósálfr spoke – a little sullenly, Ida Tueboll thought.

'There are three labours you must fulfil to make yourself . . . nice.'

And for the first time in living memory Ida Tueboll smiled a happy smile.

Ida Tueboll Begins Her Campaign

The next day was a day of signs. The first sign was posted on the wall above Ida Tueboll's head, and it said this:

'1. The Great Feast

2. The Proclamation

3. The Bringing.'

These were the three labours set her by the Ljósálfr, and this day was the day she started work on labour one: The Great Feast.

'Tis a time of rejoicing,' said the Ljósálfr from behind the light. 'A time for your people to revel and to celebrate your beneficence!'

'OK,' Ida Tueboll had said, and she had run off to find out what beneficence meant. She then listened carefully to the Ljósálfr's instructions about how to make the Feast a success, and she took appropriate action.

After the sign on her bedroom wall, she printed out hundreds of additional signs, and the additional signs said this:

'There's a Great Feast at my house.

It's tonight, from 7pm.

I expect you to attend.

All of you.

It shall be fun. There will be feasting, and music, and pets, and games.

I shall be nice.

From

Ida Tueboll.'

And she stuck them all over the school. By the time she had finished there was not a single room that did not advertise the party. She did not enter the gents' toilet herself; she made Runar Sunde do that.

Runar Sunde did as he was told. He was in Ida Tueboll's Maths class, and had made the terrible mistake of being better than her, so he was a regular target.

When the school was suitably plastered Ida Tueboll nodded to herself, and she went home to prepare the house. She started by asking her Parents to help her clear the floors for the feast. Her Parents did wonder for a moment why Ida Tueboll was having a feast, but Ida Tueboll was in no mood for conversation.

So her Parents did as they were told. They cleared out all of the downstairs rooms and replaced all of the furniture with what Ida Tueboll described as 'feast seating', and 'feast floorboards' and 'feast tables', and they covered the feast tables with solid cutlery and crockery that would withstand being dropped.

And Ida Tueboll made arrangements for the food, and prepared the feast entertainment, and she rounded up some local dogs and cats to be pets, and then she made her Parents dress up as servants, and all was ready.

And then she sat by her front door and waited.

Ida Tueboll Holds a Feast

An hour later and Ida Tueboll was still waiting. It was nearly eight pm, and she had already checked – she had said seven pm.

She considered asking the Angel in her cupboard, but she was wary of becoming overly reliant. So Ida Tueboll decided to head out and round up all the people she could find, and make them come to her Great Feast.

She reached the front gate when she heard it: the sound of hundreds and hundreds of footsteps.

She peeked along the street, and there they were – all of her schoolmates, and the teachers, and some of their parents – making their way to the Great Feast. Walking in silence – which was a sign of how excited they were, Ida Tueboll thought.

Ida Tueboll stepped back into her garden and made a snap decision to hide in the shadow cast by her Parents' enormous hedge. All the better to jump out and surprise them, which she was sure would get the Great Feast off to just the right start.

But as the footsteps approached, a single voice rose above the group, and straight away Ida Tueboll recognised it as Runar Sunde, and he said:

'If we work together I am sure that we can overpower her.'

There was no response, other than someone shushing him. And at that moment Ida Tueboll gave up on the idea of jumping out on everyone, and instead she ran to her front door and sprinted up the stairs, grabbing the iron poker as she went, intent on taking out her frustrations on the Ljósálfr rather than her guests.

'Come on,' Runar Sunde hissed, 'this is our chance!'

And Warren Trusso backhanded him across the face.

Eventually Ida Tueboll returned, without poker, and she welcomed her guests, saying:

'Welcome. Guests. Come inside for my feast.' As she made way for them she remembered to say, 'It's going to be nice.'

Ida Tueboll did her best. She smiled, she did not insult or hurt anyone. She followed the Angel's instructions to the letter. Her Parents did not stop serving all night, and the band was highly professional.

But the evening was not nice.

Firstly, her Guests were too nervous to really enjoy themselves. Every time Ida Tueboll appeared at their side they would squirm, or gasp, or, in the case of Runar Sunde, scream.

And regular screams did not help create a nice atmosphere.

Secondly, the pets did not behave as pets. Ida Tueboll had not selected the animals carefully enough, so two of the larger dogs got into a fight and upset some tables, casting a pall over much of the night.

Thirdly, the band did not create the uplifting atmosphere she was hoping for. They were just too . . . old fashioned. No one could deny that the music was beautiful, but harp, lyre and flute was the wrong combination for a modern, scared, teenage audience.

Fourthly, although the starters were delicious, a couple of the more foolhardy guests could be heard complaining about all the dates in the date stew, and the roasted grains and the barley that came with everything.

The high point of the evening was the fact that beer was on the menu for everyone, but even that may not have been entirely appropriate, given that some of the guests were twelve.

The final nail in the coffin for the evening was the centrepiece: the main course was brought into the room and paraded before being taken into the kitchen for preparation.

And that was when a couple of the vegetarians in the room decided to risk Ida Tueboll's wrath and run away. They objected to a live cow being shown around, knowing that its death was imminent.

Ida Tueboll was arrogant and dangerous, but she knew she was no fool. As she watched Mirjam Ostvedt demonstrate her customary speed, sprinting up the garden and vaulting the gate, Ida Tueboll came to the sad realisation that this night was not turning out to be nice.

She put on her best smile, ignored Runar Sunde's screams, and dismissed her guests, thanking them for coming and promising not to exact revenge on them.

She dismissed the workers and her Parents, she returned the dogs to their homes and the cow to its field, and she sloped off to bed.

She had worked hard, and the disappointment just added to her exhaustion, and Ida Tueboll could not even administer a quick torture to the Ljósálfar before she collapsed into bed.

Ida Tueboll Demands Results

The next morning things were back to normal. Ida Tueboll knew better than to apply the pain of the iron straight away, so she allowed the Ljósálfar to dig its own grave.

'So,' she said, playing carelessly with her toenail, 'how did you expect things to go?'

The Ljósálfar, which seemed to be glowing less than normal today, responded:

'Your subjects will have been impressed by your beneficence.'

'Really?' Ida Tueboll picked at her toenail with a little more force than was perhaps necessary.

'Yes. They will have departed your house with feelings of warmth and respect, countered by a little healthy fear when they saw you slaughter your steers with your bare hands.'

'Steer.'

'Sorry?'

'I could only get one. Carry on.'

'I have spoken.'

Ida Tueboll didn't respond straight away. But she did manage to pull her toenail off without necessarily realising that she was doing it. So when she left the room she trailed blood along her floor.

And when she returned she carried bricks and stones, and Ida Tueboll built a small fire pit in her bedroom, and when it was complete she lit a fire, and when it was burning bright she put three iron pokers in the fire, and she waited until they were white hot.

And the fire and the pokers were in full view of the Ljósálfar, and Ida Tueboll made sure that the Ljósálfar could see the pokers getting hot.

And Ida Tueboll noted the light flickering, and for one brief moment she was certain that it resolved itself, and the light was the head of a beautiful, proud woman with darkened brows and dark eyes, but it was quickly a flickering light again.

Ida Tueboll saw the face, and she saw it staring at the fire, and she knew that the face, however briefly there, was a scared face.

And Ida Tueboll knew that she had the Ljósálfar's complete attention. And she spoke very slowly and clearly, so that the Ljósálfar understood.

'I have completed the first labour. I have held my feast. Now – this second labour had better work, or you and I are going to have words. And some of those words might be I, and Am, and Going, and To, and Stick, and These, and Pokers, and Up, and Your, and Hole.'

Ida Tueboll jiggled the hot iron in the fire, and she knew that the Ljósálfar knew what that meant.

Ida Tueboll Arranges Her Proclamation

On the very next day Ida Tueboll went to school to prepare for her proclamation. The words of the Ljósálfar were ringing in her ear:

'Your people will hear of your wondrous deeds, and they will flock to your banner.'

'But will that make me nice?'

And the Ljósálfar did hesitate, before saying:

'Nice is what your people will love.'

And still Ida Tueboll doubted the Ljósálfar, but then the Ljósálfar demonstrated its power by turning Ida Tueboll's wooden bed into a glass bed, and Ida Tueboll nodded.

And upon the next day she made arrangements for her proclamation. She visited a photographer, and she visited a printer, and she paid for everything with her Dad's credit card.

And she made arrangements with the Head Teacher, so that the school could be organised for this wonderful event without too much intervention from Ida Tueboll, who would be too busy in the lead-up to lend a hand.

For Ida Tueboll had much to do:

She was picking up the printing.

She was finishing the list of her achievements.

And she was recruiting the team of people who would proclaim her greatness. In the end she decided on a line-up of all the kids who had wronged her in the last few months. That way they would be first to recognise her greatness, and thenceforth to recognise her niceness.

And so Ida Tueboll gathered together Mirjam Ostvedt and Warren Trusso and Lotte Bjorge and, of course, Runar Sunde. And she put them in a line on the stage, and she let them gaze at her work in wonder.

For the entire assembly hall was now covered with reminders of the greatness of Ida Tueboll.

There were banners going along and down, and there were posters, and there were pictures everywhere, and there were slogans, such as:

'All hail Ida Tueboll!'

'You will love her for she is nice!'

'Look upon her great works!'

And much, much more. And when they had finished gasping, Ida Tueboll spoke to them:

'You are the Proclaimers for today's Proclamation. When the people are assembled, you will take it in turns to walk up to the podium here, and you will take the sheet of paper with your name at the top, and you will read from it in a clear, strong voice. I shall be over there, doing the music, and I will point at each of you in turn to tell you when to go up.'

The Proclaimers looked at each other, and they shuffled their feet. And then Runar Sunde, who had been problematic recently, swallowed his fear and spoke.

'Shouldn't we practise first?'

And when Ida Tueboll stepped towards him the rest of the Proclaimers took a step backwards, and even Runar Sunde blinked nervously, but Ida Tueboll was nice now, and she smiled at him and said:

'That's a good question, Runar Sunde. But if you practise you will lose the spontaneity of the moment. You need to be as amazed by my amazing achievements and niceness as your audience. That way the sense of gratitude and love will just grow and grow.'

And with that she dismissed the Proclaimers, and she finished the preparations.

Ida Tueboll is Proclaimed

Later that day, the Proclamation of Ida Tueboll took place.

The entire school was lined up in the hall – even the Cleaners and the Catering staff. They all stared, open-mouthed, at the display in honour of Ida Tueboll.

And when she was ready, she set the music off, and began to share a slideshow of her nicest pictures with her audience. She did not notice the occasional shared glance between members of her audience.

The pictures showed different moments from Ida Tueboll's life:

Ida Tueboll as a baby

Ida Tueboll as a toddler – the hand snaking up her Dad's nose Photoshopped out

Ida Tueboll on her first day at school – with her sharpened hockey stick just out of view.

And so on. Every picture was 'amended' to make Ida Tueboll look, if not nice, then as close to nice as she could make it.

As the music came to a stop, Ida Tueboll nodded at Mirjam Ostvedt, and

Mirjam Ostvedt made her unsteady way to the podium at the front of the stage, and she began to read from the sheet with her name on it.

'I speak to you now in praise of Ida Tueboll, perhaps the nicest person you will ever know. Through difficult times and good times Ida Tueboll has been there for each and every one of us. With her . . . with her tests and her games of fun, Ida Tueboll has made everything great.'

Mirjam Ostvedt finished her speech, and she walked slowly back to her place, and if Ida Tueboll saw her shaking she did not notice it. Instead she pointed at Warren Trusso, and it was his turn to stumble to the front. He wavered over his words, and his bottom lip wobbled, but he got through them.

'Ida Tueboll saved my life. Without the . . . fun tricks that she played on me, I wouldn't be as strong as I am today. I was weak and not much fun, but then Ida Tueboll dipped me in pig's blood and made my bicycle into a dangerous trap, and now I am the . . . the happiest child alive.'

And as Warren Trusso returned to his place, even Ida Tueboll could not fail to notice the giggling she heard from the audience. Such was her surprise – no one had ever laughed at her before – that she did nothing to react. The giggling was met with some gasps too: no one ever laughed at Ida Tueboll.

The tension in the room was rising. Something was going to happen. A dam was going to burst.

Next Lotte Bjorge walked to the front of the stage. She did her best with her speech:

'Ida Tueboll is among us – rejoice! Without her strength and guidance, we would not be the happy, well-adjusted people that we are. Ida Tueboll is our friend. She is strong but she has our best interests at the heart of everything that she does.'

But Lotte Bjorge's best was not good enough. She began strongly enough – she was always in the school play – but, after stumbling over the words 'well-adjusted', she began to snort, and squeak, and tears fell from her eyes. Ida Tueboll initially thought the magnitude of the words were making Lotte Bjorge emotional, but it was soon clear that Lotte Bjorge was laughing.

And then Lotte Bjorge made wind.

And in one moment the laughter spread, and soon the entire room was laughing. There could be no mistaking it – the dam had indeed broken, and over four hundred children, teachers and support staff were all laughing.

And Ida Tueboll's big day had changed. The pictures had not changed. The intention had not changed. But people's feelings about Ida Tueboll had.

And Ida Tueboll did not know where to look. For in every direction someone was laughing. The noise, the release, meant that things got a little hysterical, and soon kids were screaming and yelling and throwing themselves around in physical fits of joy and release.

And the second endeavour was also a failure.

Runar Sunder Tidies Up

Ida Tueboll sat in the silent assembly hall, and she too was silent. Part of her was wondering if she could ever pull off the nice thing. She had just been humiliated by the entire school, and she knew that the nice thing to do would be to forgive everyone.

In fact, part of her recognised this as a key stage in her journey to acceptance: the 'all is lost' moment. With the right response, and with a lot of work, she knew that she could begin to earn people's respect, by accepting their laughter with good grace and showing willingness to learn.

That was strong.

But there was another way to be strong, and Ida Tueboll had been doing that for years and years. And as she ran through all of the different ways she could exact her revenge on every single person at the school, she realised that this way of being strong was much, much more fun.

She had even got so far as planning a repeat of her proclamation, but this time she would lead up to the event with a true reign of terror. So that, next time, the idiots would be queuing up to praise her.

And she would make each and every one of them speak for a day. With a live steer suspended over their heads. And if they stopped – if they even thought about stopping – then down the steer would come. And she would fill the steer with explosives, and nails, and . . .

But Ida Tueboll did not complete her planning, for she was interrupted by a screeching sound. She looked up to see Runar Sunde dragging a chair across the floor and adding it to a stack. Ida Tueboll watched as Runar Sunde repeated the action, again and again.

Ida Tueboll had never tidied anything away before, and so it took her a short while to realise that Runar Sunde was tidying away. All alone, without having been asked.

She called him over.

'Runar Sunde, come here.'

And Runar Sunde came over. Ida Tueboll realised that she was relieved by this: she was almost expecting him to ignore her.

'Hello, Ida Tueboll.'

'Runar Sunde, what are you doing?'

'I am tidying away, Ida Tueboll.'

'Why are you tidying away?'

'Because it's the right thing to do.'

Ida Tueboll frowned, and she stared at Runar Sunde as if seeing him for the first time.

'Runar Sunde, why are you so nice?'

Runar Sunde shrugged, and stammered, and looked flustered. Ida Tueboll realised that she often asked this question before doing something evil, so she tried again.

'No, I mean . . . how do you get to be so nice?'

Again Runar Sunde struggled to answer.

'Is it hard? Is it really hard to do?' Ida Tueboll sighed, and she said something that she had never said to anyone, ever before. 'Because I don't know how.'

Ida Tueboll looked at the floor, for she expected Runar Sunde to laugh at her – and tell everyone in the school about her failure. But he said nothing – and when she looked at him again Ida Tueboll realised that he was shaking.

'What is it?'

'Can you keep a secret, Ida Tueboll?'

Ida Tueboll shook her head. For all her faults, she was always honest.

'But I don't have any friends, Runar Sunde, so there is no-one I could tell even if I wanted to.'

And that seemed to make Runar Sunde's mind up for him, as he stepped closer and whispered to Ida Tueboll, his voice quavering as he shared his big secret.

'Being nice is hard. So, so hard. That's why I summoned a Ljósálfr to help me.'

Ida Tueboll Shares Her Secret

'How many people have been to your room, Ida Tueboll?'

Ida Tueboll shushed Runar Sunde – in truth no one other than her Parents had ever seen her room, and if anyone found out that she had brought Runar Sunde, tiny, weedy, pathetic Runar Sunde, to her secret cave of evil, well that would be it.

She would be considered weak.

But Ida Tueboll knew that Runar Sunde was strong, for he had successfully summoned a Ljósálfr, and he had used it to teach him the ways of wisdom and niceness.

That was why, when she was at her worst, he was at his best: because his Ljósálfar had behaved like a true guardian Angle, and had shown him the way before peacefully departing this world.

And Ida Tueboll had decided that being nice was the stronger thing to do, and she would learn from Runar Sunde. But first she wanted him to see her Ljósálfar, and tell her what she had been doing so wrong, because so far her Ljósálfar's advice had been rather pathetic.

So she smuggled Runar Sunde into her house, and she led him into her room, and she made him stand inside the circle, although she did not join him, as she was Ida Tueboll, and she wanted him to see how strong she was.

'Where is your Ljósálfar, Ida Tueboll?'

Ida Tueboll ignored him, for she was about to show him just that. With a flourish, she walked to her cupboard, and flung the door open. Runar Sunde peered into the cupboard.

'Where is your Ljósálfar, Ida Tueboll?'

Ida Tueboll almost gasped, fearing that her Ljósálfar had somehow escaped, but when she looked into the cupboard there it was, with its smug sleeping face. Unmistakeably the same Ljósálfar Ida Tueboll had called from the Netherworld. But Runar Sunde asked her again.

'Where is your Ljósálfar, Ida Tueboll?'

And Ida Tueboll almost fed him to her Ljósálfar, for she realised that he clearly had been lying about his own Ljósálfar. She sighed, and pointed at her Ljósálfar.

'It's there, you idiot.'

And Runar Sunde shook his head and laughed a little.

'No it's not.'

And Ida Tueboll reached out to grab Runar Sunde by the neck.

'That's not a Ljósálfar!'

Ida Tueboll stopped reaching.

'What the . . . absolute hell do you mean Runar Sunde?'

Runar Sunde laughed again, and he squeaked:

'Wait there!'

Before running from the room, leaving a very confused Ida Tueboll standing next to the cupboard which contained something that might not, in fact, be a Ljósálfar.

Ida Tueboll Learns the Terrible Truth

'Be careful! It's the only one.'

It was only minutes later that Runar Sunde had returned to Ida Tueboll's bedroom. He was panting, and he indeed confirmed that he had run all the way to his home and back.

And now, as he sat by her side, Ida Tueboll leafed through a large, hand-made book written in an obsessively neat copperplate. The printed title was The Magnus Sunde Book of Weird Things.

She saw page after page of densely written tales, packed full of descriptions, guides and tips. Every page was devoted to a particular supernatural entity. And the hand-drawn likenesses got weirder, and weirder, and weirder.

'My Dad's called all of them up at some point.' Runar Sunde was bouncing up and down on the bed, which made reading the closely-written text difficult. 'Usually he calls them up, confirms their name and then banishes them. That way there's no chance of them tricking him.'

Ida Tueboll looked at Demon after Demon, Angel after Angel, Ljósálfar after Ljósálfar and she began to wonder if she had done something even more stupid than normal.

'That's very interesting, Runar Sunde. But I can't find . . .'

Runar Sunde grabbed the Magnus Sunde Book of Weird Things from Ida Tueboll and began scrabbling through it, despite his own warning of some moments ago.

'You can't find it because you're looking in the wrong place! Look . . .'

He opened the book at the Table of Contents.

'Angels, pages 1-224. Demons, pages 225-491. Ljósálfar, pages 492-493.'

Ida Tueboll's throat went dry, as Runar Sunde moved his finger further down the page.

'Gods, pages 494-1022.'

Ida Tueboll looked up. Runar Sunde was grinning.

'Runar Sunde, are you really saying that I have a God in my cupboard? And can you stop bouncing up and down, please?'

Ida Tueboll Argues with a God

Ida Tueboll hesitated before opening the cupboard door, the warnings of Runar Sunde ringing in his ears.

'Gods are not like Angels or Demons or Ljósálfar, Ida Tueboll. They are in charge of things. Kind of like the worst Head Teacher you've ever known, but with a bigger temper and magic powers.'

Ida Tueboll had chewed up and spat out many a Head Teacher. But none of them had had magic powers before.

But she knew that she had to do this, so she screwed up her creeping fear and pushed it to the back of her mind, and she opened the cupboard door.

The face was waiting for her – a knowing smile on its face. Ida Tueboll took a moment to find her voice.

'You know what we were saying?'

'I am a God. Also your cupboard is cheap and thin.'

'Are . . . you Ereshkigal? Goddess of the Mesopotamian Underworld?'

Ereshkigal gave a regal – if ironic – nod.

'But – I wanted a Ljósálfar.'

'You asked for Ereshkigal.'

'I asked for a Ljósálfar.'

Ereshkigal frowned, a look of annoyance…

'You asked for eaarrgh splurgle gurgle Ereshkigaal.'

Ida Tueboll gasped. The Goddess had just repeated her cough exactly.

'Eaarrgh and Splurgle Gurgle no longer exist on any plane. But I do. Have you completed your labours?'

Ida Tueboll shook her head. She was scared to say much else.

'But you will still complete them?'

Ida Tueboll thought about this. She thought about that bargain.

'If I finish them, will you take me to the Underworld?'

'That was the bargain. Have you completed your labours?'

'But if I can go to the Underworld . . . I can come back right?'

The Goddess smiled again. Ida Tueboll balled her fists.

'You said I could come back!'

And now Ereshkigal got angry, and her voice blew Ida Tueboll off her feet.

'I said you could try! But know this, fool with an iron stick: no human has ever left the Underworld without my help. And for your temerity and your stupidity know this: I shall fasten on you the eye of death. I shall speak against you the word of wrath. I shall utter against you the cry of guilt. I shall turn you into a corpse, a piece of rotting meat, and I shall hang you from a hook on the wall.'

Ida Tueboll Comes Up with a Plan

The next day, and the day after, Ida Tueboll tried to pretend that she was not going to be taken to the Underworld against her will.

But it was not easy. Ereshkigal was now displaying her full powers. During the first lunch break, all of the other Kids lined up to tell Ida Tueboll, in the voice of the Goddess, that she was damned forever.

Not even Ida Tueboll could ignore that. And when the birds and the dogs on the way home queued up to say the same thing, she remembered a conversation she had once had with Warren Trusso.

'Tell me, Warren Trusso,' she had said, as he hung upside down from the gym bars, 'how do you feel when you see me walking towards you?'

'Well,' Warren Trusso had said, 'do you know that feeling when every single part of your body feels like it hates you?'

'No,' Ida Tueboll had said.

'Well that's it. I call it dread.'

And Ida Tueboll now knew what dread felt like. Having friendly little puppies march up to you and tell you your life was forfeit? That was dread.

So Ida Tueboll did what she had never done before in her life. She asked another human being for help.

And Runar Sunde was happy to help. He was happy to do lots of things. He did not seem overly worried that Ida Tueboll was about to lose her eternal soul, but she put that down to his naivety. They met in the local park, far away from prying eyes and ears.

She asked him about the bargain she had made.

'What if I just don't complete the final task?'

'Well that depends, Ida Tueboll. What is the final task?'

'I need to bring a good friend to my house, and I need to ask them to tell the . . . Goddess what a nice person I am. And if they lie she will know.'

'Well that's going to be hard, isn't it? Nobody likes you.'

154

Ida Tueboll stopped herself from knocking Runar Sunde's head off, because he was naïve. And he was right.

'But what if I never do it?'

Runar Sunde shrugged.

'Then you will have an increasingly angry Goddess in your cupboard, who will probably do whatever is in her power to make your life miserable, until completing your tasks and going to the Underworld is the nicest option. And she's powerful too – really powerful, my Dad . . .'

'OK! I get the picture.' Ida Tueboll sat back and peered at the sky. She felt that dread coming again, particularly when a small sparrow flittered onto the bench next to her and piped:

'You will be drawn behind the Brahmin Bull of Stink for all eternity!'

She turned back to Runar Sunde.

'Is the Underworld that bad?'

Runar Sunde thought for a moment, before saying:

'Well, Ida Tueboll, it's not wonderful. But it's not like Hell. In Hell you'll get burned and cut into bits. In the Underworld it's more like . . . you'll be surrounded by dust, and all the people are shadows, so you'll be spending, like, eternity, in the company of the shades of the dead. And if they catch you they'll probably drag you behind the Brahmin Bull of Stink.'

'Is there no hope?'

Runar Sunde pursed his lips, then he rummaged around in his rucksack, threw away a mouldy banana skin, and passed an old book to Ida Tueboll.

'Read the second story from the end.'

Ida Tueboll did read the second story from the end. Then she returned the book to Runar Sunde.

'That's probably the stupidest thing I've ever read. And it's not true.'

'Really?'

Runar Sunde read the book again. And then he face-palmed himself.

'Do people actually do that?'

'Sorry,' said Runar Sunde, returning the book to Ida Tueboll, 'that was that vile story The Nine Rules of the Nisse written by the Mad Arab Matthew White. I meant the third from the end. The Story of Inanna and Her Journey to the Underworld.'

Ida Tueboll did read the third story from the end. Then she returned the book to Runar Sunde.

'Do you think it might work?'

'It's in the book.' He showed her the cover. It was called 'The Book of True Stories'.

Ida Tueboll pondered...

'So all I have to do is get someone to go willingly into the underworld in my place?'

'Yes!'

Ida Tueboll pondered some more.

'And how willingly do they have to go?'

'It's a verbal bargain! As long as they say they'll do it – then they are willing!'

Ida Tueboll pondered for a long, long time. And then she turned to Runar Sunde with a big smile on her face.

'Runar Sunde, will you come to the Goddess and tell her how great I am?'

Ida Tueboll Makes the Final Bargain

Ida Tueboll stood outside her bedroom door. She turned to Runar Sunde, who jumped nervously on the spot.

'Runar Sunde, can you stop jumping up and down, please? You'll break the floorboards.'

Runar Sunde stopped jumping up and down, but that just meant that his eyebrows started to jiggle. Ida Tueboll placed a hand on his shoulder.

'Don't worry, you'll be just fine. Have you memorised the words?'

Runar Sunde nodded, and Ida Tueboll opened the door to her bedroom.

She tried not to gasp, but she did gasp, and so did Runar Sunde.

Ereshkigal, Goddess of the Underworld, had grown. Her queenly face now hovered above, around and over the cupboard. And her once black eyes were now flickering with a flame which, on a more happy occasion, Ida Tueboll would have dismissed as clichéd.

Ida Tueboll dragged a reluctant Runar Sunde into the room, and she forced herself to look the clichéd – but still very, very scary – Goddess in her enormous face.

'Ereshkigal, Goddess of the Underworld, I come here to complete my last task.'

The Goddess said nothing. Ida Tueboll continued.

'I have brought a witness to pay testimony to my niceness. Runar Sunde! Complete the testimony.'

Runar Sunde stepped forward. And, as Ida Tueboll later thought, he made a very good fist of remembering the words she had given him.

'I, Runar Sunde, do hereby bear witness that Ida Tueboll is the nicest person in the world. You will know that I speak the truth, and if I lie then may I be taken to the Underworld in her place.'

Runar Sunde stepped back, and Ida Tueboll felt a pang of regret. She had counted on his naivety, and it had worked – but this did not make her feel good.

Ereshkigal screwed up her gigantic face, and she bellowed.

'IDA TUEBOLL! You are a snake in the grass.'

The Goddess turned to Runar Sunde.

'You, little human, are lying. I, Ereshkigal, Goddess of the Underworld, Queen of the Dead, see all, and I see that Ida Tueboll is not the nicest person in the world. In fact she is not the nicest person in this room. And even if she were the only person in the room she would not be the nicest person in the room. And thereby, by your lies and your statement, you must take her place and be dragged to the Underworld.'

Runar Sunde turned to Ida Tueboll. His little eyes filled with tears.

'What . . . what have you done, Ida Tueboll?'

Ida Tueboll could not look at Runar Sunde. In her 14 years upon the planet she had hacked, tricked, suppressed, bullied, tripped, burned and yelled her path through humanity, leaving thousands of people broken, terrified and fearful.

And in all that time she had never once regretted it – these people were, after all, weak.

But now, as she avoided Runar Sunde's despairing gaze, she finally felt regret. Regret that the one time someone tried to do something truly nice for her, she had responded by condemning him to a life of eternity in the Underworld.

And the enormity of her crimes came to her, channelled by the words of Runar Sunde.

'Ida Tueboll. I thought . . . we were friends.'

Ida Tueboll wanted to answer, and wanted to make Runar Sunde feel happy again, but the Goddess spoke first, and sneered at them both.

'No matter! Now I return to my home, and your so-called friend has condemned you to join me. Come – and leave this weak human behind.'

The Goddess's head began to shrink, and Runar Sunde screamed as he felt himself being dragged across the floor towards the cupboard.

But Ida Tueboll had other ideas.

She shouted at the Goddess, and such was the power and anger in her voice that even Ereshkigal paused.

'Wait!'

There was silence. And Ida Tueboll turned from the cupboard, bent over her bed for a moment, and then turned back to the Goddess, buttoning up her jumper as she did so.

'Take me.'

Ereshkigal blinked.

'Take me. I reject my trick, and I want to be taken to the Underworld for all eternity.'

The Goddess opened her mouth. But Ida Tueboll cut her off.

'Don't waste our time. You know you want me and not him. Take me.'

It did not take Ereshkigal more than a fraction of a second to make her decision. And as her head began to shrink, and Ida Tueboll felt herself being pulled across the floor, she smiled at an amazed Runar Sunde. And she spoke her final words on this earth.

'Be nice, Runar Sunde.'

Ida Tueboll Goes to the Underworld

Ida Tueboll opened her eyes.

It made no difference. She could see nothing. She was in a pitch dark space, but by the building of the air pressure around her Ida Tueboll knew that the pitch dark space was speeding downwards.

And by the feeling of cold and the smell of dry beside her, she knew that she stood in the presence of a Goddess. And from the darkness, and all around her, Ereshkigal spoke.

'You will regret your generosity Ida Tueboll, when you reach my home.'

Ida Tueboll grinned to herself.

'So tell me – are you the Queen of the Dead?'

'Of course I am the Queen of the Dead!'

'But not the Queen of the Recently Dead. More the Queen of the . . . Wispy, Faded Spirits of the People from Your Time.'

Ida Tueboll felt the Goddess hesitate.

'The Queen of the Weak.'

'I am the Queen of the Dead! And I shall enjoy the pain and the suffering I shall inflict upon you Ida Tueboll!'

And in response Ida Tueboll reached into her jumper and pulled out the iron poker she had hidden there, and she hefted it in her hands. And she felt the Goddess shrink away from her. And when Ida Tueboll spoke, she could feel the fear coming from her opponent.

'I think not.'

And the Dead never knew what hit them.

About the authors

A J Dalton

A J Dalton (the 'A' is for Adam) has been an English language teacher as far afield as Egypt, the Czech Republic, Thailand, Slovakia, Poland and Manchester University. He has lived in Manchester since 2003, but has a conspicuous Cockney accent, as he was born in Croydon on a dark night, when strange stars were seen in the sky.

He is the best-selling fantasy author of The Book of Orm (2015), Empire of the Saviours (2012), Gateway of the Saviours (2013), Tithe of the Saviours (2014), Necromancer's Gambit (2008), Necromancer's Betrayal (2009) and Necromancer's Fall (2010). He maintains the Metaphysical Fantasy website (www.ajdalton.eu), where there is plenty to interest fantasy fans and there is advice for aspiring authors.

Sammy H.K Smith

Sammy H.K Smith lives in the sunny county of Oxfordshire with her husband, her son, and a menagerie of animals. In Search of Gods and Heroes is her debut novel, and the first of the Children of Nalowyn series. She has contributed to several anthologies, including The Nun & Dragon by Fox Spirit Books and Strange Tales from the Scriptorian Vaults by Kristell Ink.

Between working full-time in the police as a detective, running Grimbold Books, raising a family and writing, she is working towards her degree in English Language & Literature with the OU. She enjoys reading (obviously!), mythology, music, films, and a host of other uninteresting hobbies.

She can be found on Facebook: www.facebook.com/sammyhksmith

Michael Bowman

Michael Bowman has been described as witty, entertaining and compelling, but when asked to describe himself he usually dodges the question and tells you a story, instead. There's evidence that he's studied everything from Kung Fu to carpentry, and wood cutter ants to naval history. What we do know is that he was a bathroom salesman, that he is a biology graduate and that he was once chased by an angry hippo in Tanzania.

When not running for his life he hammers away at his ratty old Microsoft keyboard and brews the strong tea that fuels his new website, Life described (www.lifedescribed.com). He's got a lot to say about how to get published and plans to follow his own advice with the imminent release of his first novel. In the meantime he shares his views on everything from natural history to space travel. So if you liked his story 'The Lucky Ones' please stop by his website to leave a comment because, as Charles Buxton said, silence is the severest criticism.

Andrew Coulthard

Andrew Coulthard first saw the light of day on the wind-lashed eastern coast of Northumbria. He then spent most of his childhood and youth in the western shadow of the highland boundary fault. Since 1990 he has dwelt north of the land of the Geats – where it can get very cold.

By day he is a language training consultant and translator, by night a writer of weird fiction, slipstream, horror, scifi and fantasy. Andrew's short fiction has been appeared in anthologies published by Eibonvale, The Alchemy Press, MorbidbookS, Oneiros Books and Omnium Gatherum. He has also featured in Trevor Denyer's Hellfire Crossroads and The Ironic Fantastic. His Swedish work is published by Affront Förlag.

When not writing he spends time with his kids, explores heroic landscapes and enjoys surfeits of good food and drink - sometimes all at once.

Caimh McDonnell

Caimh McDonnell is an award-winning stand-up comedian, author and writer of televisual treats.

In his time on the British stand-up circuit, he has firmly established himself as the white-haired Irishman whose name nobody can pronounce. He regularly supports Sarah Millican on tour and has also done stand-up tours of the Far East, the Middle East and, once, the near east (Norwich). He brings a new stand-up show to the Edinburgh festival pretty much every year, mainly as an excuse to eat things that've been deep fried.

He has just published his second novel The Day That Never Comes, which is the follow-up to his critically acclaimed debut A Man with One of Those Faces. Both are set in his hometown of Dublin and add a demented comedic twist to the crime genre. He is also the co-creator with fellow comic Gary Delaney of the live show and podcast 'Panelbeaters' that is taking the comedy world by storm. You can find out more at www.panelbeaterscomedy.com if you really want.

When not doing all that, Caimh is in great demand as a writer for TV. He has recently worked on the hit BBC2 show 'The Sarah Millican Television Programme' and written for comics on 'Mock the Week' and 'Have I Got News for You'. He also works as a children's TV writer and was BAFTA nominated for the CBBC animated series 'Pet Squad', which he created.

All-in-all, he manages to keep himself busy. Find him if you dare: www.white-hairedirishman.com.

Matthew White

Matt White's first novel, North by North Ryde, was published in Australia in 1999. He enjoyed the process so much that he rushed out his next story, The Nine Rules of the Nisse, in time for the 2015 release of The Book of Orm. He also writes film scripts: his award-winning short films have been shown around the world, including at the LA Film Festival – LA in this case standing for 'Lewiston-Auburn', whilst his co-written feature film, The Final Haunting (2014), was also shown at international film festivals. Matt is currently working on a YA novel, and his latest film script, Farmers vs Monsters, was recently long-listed for the 2016 Euroscript Competition. Matt lives at the bottom of a valley, and keeps trying to ride his new bike up the sides. He's not made it to the top yet. You can follow Matt on Twitter via @treeandtroll.

Acknowledgements

A whole slew of people have helped put together the The Book of Angels. I'd like to thank . . .

Joanne Hall and Sammy H.K Smith of Kristell Ink, whose tolerance and good faith are equally rare amongst publishers

Evelinn Enoksen (www.facebook.com/enoksen.art), who's done a cover that is as scary as it is heavenly for this book

Michael Bowman, Sammy H.K Smith (again), Andrew Coulthard, Caimh McDonnell and Matthew White, my inspiring co-authors, who have contributed their work, hearts and minds in return for a small pile of groats

Mum and Dad, who continue to support the literary ambitions of their son against all good reason and common sense

Nadine West, my beautiful wife, whose only flaw is that she writes better than me

Peter Sutton, a valued supporter of Grimbold Books and its imprints

and all those fantasy fans who keep insisting it's all worth it!

I humbly salute you all!

A Selection of Other Titles from Kristell Ink

The Book of Orm by A J Dalton

This exciting new collection brings together the writing talents of international fantasy author A J Dalton, Nadine West (Bridport Anthology) and Matt White (prize-winning scriptwriter). Magic, myth and heroic mayhem combine in a world that is eerily familiar yet beautifully liberating.

In Search of Gods and Heroes by Sammy H.K Smith

Buried in the scriptures of Ibea lies a story of rivalry, betrayal, stolen love, and the bitter division of the gods into two factions. This rift forced the lesser deities to pledge their divine loyalty either to the shining Eternal Kingdom or the darkness of the Underworld. When a demon sneaks into the mortal world and murders an innocent girl to get to her sister Chaeli, all pretence of peace between the gods is shattered. For Chaeli is no ordinary mortal, she is a demi-goddess, in hiding for centuries, even from herself. But there are two divine brothers who may have fathered her, and the fate of Ibea rests on the source of her blood. Chaeli embarks on a journey that tests her heart, her courage, and her humanity. Her only guides are a man who died a thousand years ago in the Dragon Wars, a former assassin for the Underworld, and a changeling who prefers the form of a cat. The lives of many others – the hideously scarred Anya and her gaoler; the enigmatic and cruel Captain Kerne; the dissolute Prince Dal; and gentle seer Hana – all become entwined. The gods will once more walk the mortal plane spreading love, luck, disease, and despair as they prepare for the final, inevitable battle. In Search of Gods and Heroes, Book One of Children of Nalowyn, is a true epic of sweeping proportions which becomes progressively darker as the baser side of human nature is explored, the failings and ambitions of the gods is revealed, and lines between sensuality and sadism, love and lust are blurred.

Fear The Reaper by Tom Lloyd

All Shell has ever wanted was a home, a place to belong. But now an angel of the God has tracked her down, intent on using her to hunt the demon that once saved her. The journey will take her into the dead place beyond the borders of the world, there to face her past and witness the coming of a new age.

A stand-alone novella from the author of The Twilight Reign series and Moon's Artifice.

www.kristell-ink.com